Isdal Woman

Chapter 1
Bergen, Norway, February 5, 1971

Just before noon, a group of twelve, most of them police investigators wearing dark, worn-out coats and hats, stood in silence around a beautiful coffin between the bare, tall trees at the Møllendal burial ground in Bergen. Four carriers and two female singers stood right behind the group of men.

Before and after the Catholic burial ritual, bleak and dutiful voices joined the priest and two singers as they sang two verses of a Norwegian psalm called *O take my hands* (Så ta da mine hender).

The chapel had been decorated with flowers and two large decorations of carnations and tulips lay on top of the coffin. The funeral was kept secret and no reporters or unauthorized people were allowed to be present.

The priest held a beautiful speech based on the Psalm of David number 130 and spoke about the unknown woman who was buried in a foreign country with none of her relatives present.

The unknown woman was to receive a nameless grave with the following inscription: G.L. 00, number 00, grave 01 at the Møllendal graveyard. The coffin was zinc-lined to make relocation easier in case the woman's relatives were to be located.

The group sang the Norwegian psalm *Oh Stay With Me* (O bli hos meg), which was followed by musical pieces played on an organ and a violin. Finally the two women sang a renowned Norwegian psalm, *Lead mild light* (Leid milde ljos).

The conducted his final blessing and the service ended. The participants walked out into the beautiful winter weather among the tombs that still had the remains of flowers and wreaths from the Christmas season.

Two investigators, Seland and Berger, walked in silence alongside the chief of the Criminal Police Center and nodded dutifully at his statements on their way towards the cars in the parking lot.

Another priest stood in the chapel doorway receiving the next of kin pertaining to the funeral starting at quarter past twelve. A middle-aged bald man with a wide overcoat left the entrance to the chapel and slipped out unnoticed among the new arrivals. He had snug into a small room where the priest kept his personal things and the burial testimony. With the little instamatic camera he used to photograph prescriptions at the pharmacy, where he worked, he now had a photograph of the page in the church book that confirmed the funeral and the details around it.

Isdalen Valley, November 1970

A little over two months before the funeral, on November 29, 1970, Professor Sund and his two daughters were hiking in the Isdalen valley, just southeast of the Bergen city center. That Sunday morning, low clouds hang over the valley and the temperature was only 5 degrees Celsius.

On the way down Isdalen valley, at the entrance to Smalisdalen valley and just north of Dødsdalen (Death valley), as it was called among the villagers, the elder daughter, who had gone slightly off the path, caught up with the other two rather startled. - "There's a human being there, daddy", she cried out fearfully. Even if the professor was startled as well, he pulled his daughter close to comfort her while he talked to her in a soothing voice. - "Take it easy, calm down", he said before he told her to wait with her sister, while he went in the direction that she had come from.

In a small mound of stones at the edge of the flickering morning light, a woman's body lay naked and burned. The professor immediately felt discomfort, at the sight of the body. He found himself in a surreal situation, with the smell of burned clothes and hair; the tall dark trees around him; and the unsettling sight of the stiffened and collapsed soot-burned figure. The woman was obviously dead and it seemed as if she had been lying there for some time. It stank of old burnt odors and the flames were obviously extinguished a while ago. Nevertheless, he got shivers down his spine and unconsciously looked around as if to look for the perpetrator. - "Bloody hell", he mumbled, trying to shake off the uncomfortable feeling, before returning to his two daughters. Aware that they were not to touch anything at the scene, the professor explained to them that they should go get help immediately. The three of them followed the path into the valley without meeting other hikers and went straight home to call in and report their find to the police.

Police officers Berger and Seland, who were in charge, responded without hesitation and urgently sent a car to Professor Sunds home to gather more information. A patrol car was also sent to the intersection of Isdalen valley right away.

A constable was placed at the entrance to the valley to prevent unwanted traffic from entering. The criminal chief and the forensic pathologist, Professor Dr. Garder at the Pathological Institute, were the first to get informed. Professor Garder was experienced, professional and considered highly skilled in criminal matters, at least by the local police.

A short while later, Professor Sund guided Berger and Seland and a group of other officials and police officers from the technical department to the location where his daughter had found the body in Isdalen.

During the afternoon the officials secured the place where the body was found and placed guards, as the body was not to be moved until the following day. Upon request from the coroner's office, a pathology expert from the Gade Institute was appointed to perform the autopsy.

Due to the unusual circumstances surrounding the case, the chief criminal investigator later ordered that the Bergen police murder investigation committee would be summoned to meet at his office as soon as possible. Two police officers, Haktor Seland and Paul Berge both had years of experience in solving criminal cases. They were ordered to conduct the investigation and thus gained access to all resources available. Seland was put in charge of the investigation.

Both were family men like most of the police officers in Bergen. They were both skilled and confident investigators that the chief of police had promoted and kept out of the regular shift duty routine.

Seland used to joke about the fact that Berger, who was born and bred in a place called Sundfjord, after many years in the service had now turned into an ordinary guy from Bergen. Although small in built, Berger was powerful and had a gentle mood. He was a stark contrast to the tall, slender and sarcastic Seland, which is why some people referred to them as "Whole and Half". Despite the nicknames, they were both self-confident, highly result-oriented and seemed to possess an internal authority that came from having successfully solved several cases at the Bergen Police force.

Seland and Berger performed their duties in a way that seemed almost automatic. They followed a routine and were very much "by-the-book" so to speak. As routine would suggest, later that same evening, the Criminal Police Center, Kripos, was informed about the case. From December 1-3, information on the case was sent to police chiefs all over Norway and to Stockholm, Sweden and Copenhagen, Denmark.

Suitcases that had been left at the railway storage center in Bergen were linked to the deceased. Even if it seemed likely that the two suitcases had belonged to the deceased, Seland had doubts about making any discoveries related to the suitcases public at the time. There could be clues in the suitcases that could be diminished if their discovery became public. Despite his doubts, Kripos insisted and published the information.
- "There is hardly anything we can do about that. Besides, those Kripos guys should know what they are doing, right?" Seland said to Berger with a resigned grimace on his face. A short while later, Kripos sent out the following:

"Criminal Police Centre, December 3, 1970, telex No. 9627/28/70
An unknown female found.
«Sunday 29.11.70 at 13:15, the body of a young woman was found on a hiking trail in the Isdalen valley of Bergen in Norway. The body had been exposed to strong heat and the clothes are completely or partially burned. The body also has significant burns.
Description: Approx. 30-40 years, 164 centimeter tall, slender, strong hips, nicely built, long brown-black hair in a ponytail with a ribbon tied around it; ribbon with light blue drawings with white on a dark-blue bottom. A small, round face, brown eyes, small ears, teeth with many restorations, and several molars have gold crowns that are common in the East and some places in southern and central Europe. Fourteen of the teeth are completely or partially rooted, among these two wisdom teeth in the lower jaw and a space between the two upper front teeth.

A longer description of the clothing and belongings found on the spot followed, such as that of 1/2 a bottle of Curacau and an eyelet from a passport found under the corpse.

«Two relatively large suitcases were found at the luggage storage area at the Bergen railroad station, one brown with a belt around it, and the other one yellow. They were deposited into storage on November 23, and contain, among other things, the following outer garments: A light fur coat and a light trench coat with a fur collar.
Included in the findings associated with the suitcases was also a tube of steroid cream from the Trane pharmacy in Bergen, where the date and the name of the doctor who prescribed it, were scraped off. There was also a tube of cream by "Baranne France"; a paper tissue with the imprint "London" on it; matches

branded "Versandhaus Beate Uhse Flensburg"; a plastic bag labeled "Nicolshoes Roma"; sports shoes branded "Salamander"; a post card with a Norwegian winter motif; a laboratory knife marked "Inox"; Perfumes from "Jaques Esterel"; several wigs, an envelope marked "Hotel Regina Genève"; and Dagbladet (a Norwegian newspaper) from November 21 displaying an article about the Montessori school in Rome. The suitcases are believed to belong to the deceased. In addition, a large amount of clothing and items on which the brand tags have been removed. It has not been possible to discover the woman's identity. Fingerprints are included. The deceased did not use credit cards.

Related information can be communicated per telex here. «111166b ipol No"

Even though Kripos wanted to control the flow of information, Seland had managed to convince them that there were some details about the discovery and the suitcases that could damage the investigation if it became public at the time.

The message therefore stated nothing about the fact that there were no usable fingerprints on the bags or any of the items in them. All prints that had been on smooth surfaces, such as bottles, had obviously been carefully removed.

The only exception had been fragments of a print on a pair of broken eyeglasses placed at the top of one suitcase. Although the impression was poor and difficult to compare with the burned impressions on the body, they seemed to have found it to be a fit for one of the little fingers of the deceased. Thus, together with the investigative management, they concluded that the suitcases belonged to the person found dead in the Isdalen valley.

The police in Bergen also sent a description of the woman to all hotels and accommodations in the city center in an attempt to acquire additional information. The woman was described as having had her dark hair in a ponytail, tied with a ribbon, wearing a leather cap, a quilted jacket with a belt, a dark blue sweater, a colorful woolen shawl, socks and semi-high laced rubber boots from the Norwegian brand "Kjendis". Likely carrying a blue nylon lady's umbrella.

The following day, the front page of the Bergen newspaper was filled with headlines, mysterious interpretations and pictures from the scene where the body had been found.

Moscow, December 1, 1970

The first inquiries of information from the Bergen police related to the discovery of an unknown dead woman were immediately picked up by the Russian Embassy in Oslo and forwarded to Moscow, on Tuesday, December 1, 1970. In Moscow, all available intelligence officers were directed to capture any information on the case from Norway and northern Europe.

Sergei Tonkin, who led operations at KGB headquarters in Moscow, tore the paper out of the operator's hands and read it with great interest. - "Excellent! We've done it!" he exclaimed, as soon as he had skimmed through the message. He held his head high and turned triumphantly towards the others in the room, a man and a woman, while giving the operator a pat on the arm:

"Still no clues!! In any case, send a thank you and confirm with Captain Voltov that we re ready" Tonkin had victory written all over his face as he walked out the door to brief is party secretary.

Soon after, the coded message "Isotopsy" went out and was confirmed as received alf an hour later by the embassy in Stockholm and from the USSR's Vostok submarine om an unknown position in the Baltic Sea. On board the submarine, captain Voltov odded with satisfaction while the course was immediately redirected to Gdansk in oland.

ergen, December 1970

few days after the woman's body was found, the police was already inclined to assume nat she was not Norwegian. Both on December 4 and additionally on December 8, a oded and more comprehensive description was sent to Interpol's Zone 1 and 2 offices, ncluding: Helsinki, Brussels, The Hague, Lisbon, London, Luxembourg, Madrid, Rome, ienna, Wiesbaden, Switzerland, Paris BCN and SG, and Belgrade. In addition, inquiries vere sent to CID Jerusalem, Romania, Greece, Yugoslavia, Lebanon and the FBI in New ork.

The fragments of her fingerprints were included, although these were of poor uality because of her burned fingertips.

The police received information on a certain "Fenella Lorc" who had come to ergen via Stavanger from Geneva.

A local artist, Audun Hetland, was asked to make a drawing of the woman on the asis of the information provided by pathologists and additionally by descriptions from otel personnel. The drawing was then copied and distributed along with the inquiries o the Interpol.

An imprint of the woman's dental anatomy was sent to dental registers and ental journals across major parts of the world. For example Tribuna Odontologica rgentina; Deutsche Zahn-Mund; K. Escheverri Columbia; Basauri Lima, Odontoiatria ladrid; Faculty of Rio; L'editrice Scient. Italy; and Inform Dentaire Paris.

Despite the international search, the answers were generally negative. Nobody vas able to identify the woman through dental records, nor did they find a match in nissing person's registers.

Interpol in Wiesbaden checked the data against Ulricke Meinhof, the Bader-Meinhof organization, but unsuccessfully as there were no usable fingerprints.

Pressure from the media on the investigators rose incrementally from day to day. ournalists from all over Scandinavia called in or visited Bergen in the hopes of equiring more information on the case.

The local newspapers were covered in stories related to the case as they managed o pick up more recent information than the others. The investigators were surprised by he ability of the media people to obtain new information. One of the headlines struck eland and Berger the most:

INTENTIONAL ATTEMPTS TO ERADICATE THE ISDAL WOMAN'S IDENTITY?"

- "They are damn unreliable", exclaimed Seland. He and Berger stood together, looking t the newest edition of the local newspaper to see what the journalists had written.

–"Typical!" replied Berger. "All the work and struggle we go through to solve the case and it gets lost in one single foolish newspaper entry. I wish they would keep silent for now and allow us some time to do our jobs."

Seland nodded seemingly in agreement. However, without having much experience with the press in such big cases, he felt somewhat proud to be the center of attention. In addition, he even had several of the local journalists in the palm of his hand, something he often made use of in small cases to promote police interests.

At the moment Seland had other worries besides media reports. He was more concerned with getting Professor Garder to elaborate on his findings, in addition to the brief preliminary autopsy report he had sent.

"The woman was found in a remote place where people usually do not go. In rough terrain between several large stones, she lay on her back on a slight slope with her head at the bottom. The arms were in "boxer stance." There were severe burns and the skin was sooty. The woman was well built, 164 tall and weighed 5. kg. The legs were partially burned through to the bone. The head was almost black and only leftovers remained of the hair on the back of the neck. The abdominal skin was relatively intact and there were clear marks for a brassiere with straps over the shoulders. The tongue, throat, and esophagus were normal. The heart weighed 310 gr., the lungs 840 gr., and the liver 1370 gr. The uterus was normal, outer orifice of the uterus round, and the woman had most likely never given birth. The gastric bag contained a gray-green viscous liquid and grained white material as if from pills. No morbid changes were found. In the large throat muscle on the right side, bleeding from the tendon attachment and 4-5 cm up in the muscle was found."

Seland had sat down with the report late in the afternoon and reacted to the pathologists' senseless descriptions. However, he knew from experience how important it was that the document objectively reflected all of the conditions that could affect the investigation. After skimming relatively quickly through the first details and the photographs, he radiated with excitement at the pathologists own final summary and judgment of the survey. The so-called discussion and conclusion in the report, provided him with some insight:

"The amount of alcohol in the blood was small and irrelevant to the onset of death. The traces of the sleeping aid Fenemal that was detected in the blood probably came from 12 tablets of medium strength, taken 3-4 hours before her death. The tablets could lead to mild relaxation. Twice as many lead to unconsciousness. The stomach content showed that more tablets were taken just before death. Soot particles in the trachea indicate that the deceased was alive when the fire occurred. The age of the deceased is estimated to be closer to 25 than 30 years."

"They measured high values of carbon dioxide in the blood", Seland said as he lay back in the chair and blew a long "phoooo" as he stared up at the ceiling seemingly lost in his own thought. - "This is eventually going straight to hell", he exclaimed after a while.

ater in the investigation, chemical analysis of blood, urine and stomach contents were available from the Toxicological Institute. The forensic doctor summarized approximately as follows:

> "The forensic findings indicate suicide. It cannot be known whether the fire damage was due to her pouring gasoline over herself or if it was an accident. Although there are no external marks on the skin, a severe bleeding occurred in the large throat muscle on the right side to where the collarbone is attached. This must have occurred by blows or bumps against a blunt object. It may be due to a strike of a hand, for example, a punch on the throat. However, the conclusion is that the deceased, in a dull state of mind, on her way through the woods on a rugged, slippery terrain, must have stumbled and fallen against a tree branch."

n the report from the institute, carbon monoxide in the blood was not mentioned. In he final summary from the medical crew it was postulated that the previous local carbon oxide content analysis could be too high.

The incident report from police officer Jan Henriksen showed that the whole body was burned by fire. It was reddish-brown and gave a convincing impression of being affected by a short-lived but intense fire on the surface. The fact that there was a print of a rubber boot in the white ash by the right knee of the body, or that the deceased had been dressed, apart from the blue sailing boots of which the remains were found, was considered unimportant. Only the remains of a passport were found. This lay under the body, among the remains of the campfire, which was considered to have been burned before the greater fire was lit, because parts of the clothes on the backside under the body, on the hip and bottom, were not burned. The strap on the solar watch that was found next to her was burnt, also on the backside. The fact that it had stopped at 12:30 probably was due to the hit it had suffered.

Although Henriksen had experience both as an investigator and a technician, this case was unusual. He was completely comfortable with surrounding himself with dead bodies. Like everyone in the department, he was taken to the autopsy unit early in his career to get used to death and to have the necessary confidence to be able to handle difficult situations. Those who did not tolerate this were quickly given other tasks.

Most of the cases he had participated in were related to natural death. Fire and accidents were a rare cause of death. The scene of the naked burned woman in Isdalen valley was different. He already had his personal interpretation on the events that had taken place. He believed that the position of the body, gave the impression that she could have been a victim of foul play. However, he did not write a new report, as the pathologists believed that the fire itself probably would have made her take the boxing position. He was of a different opinion, especially when he considered that the fingerprints were removed from all of her belongings found in the suitcases. The pathology report and the significant interest from Kripos and POT, with a clear demand to reach a conclusion in the matter as quickly as possible, weighed heavily. The report from the National Institute of Public Health, with the analysis of the woman's stomach and blood, played no larger role than was expected. The first phase of the case was closed and the police committee concluded suicide as a probable cause of death.

Bergen, December 1970

The woman was still unidentified and not reported missing by anyone, either in Norway or abroad. The tension in the local community and in the press was tremendous.

In the provisionally established research center in Bergen people were quite confused and overwhelmed by all the surprising data that rolled in as the events in the case were laid out.

Requests to hotels, passport offices and airline companies resulted in extensive information relating to who the woman could have been.

Two postcards and a note with numbers and letters were found in one of the suitcases. These were sent to the defense department for decoding. A series of interviews were conducted with witnesses.

Berger, who, in the early stages of the investigation, leaned more towards the probability that the case was local and Norwegian and that the woman most likely had escaped from an institution, failed to conceal a nervous eruption after the discovery of a coded note. - "Fuck me! This is all too fucked up. We are in the middle of this big fucking case!"

The investigation determined that the woman must have had at least four different identities. Fenella Lorc, who had stayed at the hotel St. Svithun in Stavanger from November 9-18, turned out to be the same as Elisabeth Leenhouwfr, a guest at Rosenkrantz Hotel in Bergen the night pertaining to November 19, who then moved to Hordaheimen hotel the next day. Leenhouwfr stayed at Hordaheimen until she checked out of the hotel on November 23 and left in a taxi.

A passenger list from SAS airlines showed that a woman named L. Selling, who was in accordance with the description, traveled from Trondheim to Stavanger via Oslo on November 9. The samples of the handwriting conducted by the hotel in Stavanger, SAS and Rosenkranz hotels showed that this was the same woman who was registered on November 9 at St. Svithun as Fenella Lorc. Hotel Bristol in Trondheim had a guest named Vera Jarle, from November 6-9, which by the descriptions and comparisons of writing samples, was concluded to be the same person as L. Selling.

All of the hotels shared that the woman had changed rooms just after arrival on account that she did not want to stay in rooms with a balcony.

One of the military's most successful code experts from the war concluded that the list from the suitcase with numbers and letters, described a travel route with dates and the first letter of a temporary place of residence.

Further analysis indicated that the same woman had also visited Norway in March. Passport checks and alien forms from March were checked against the decoded list and names were checked against those that had already been discovered.

The small numbers and letters on the list were set up approximately as follows:

10 m a 23- a 29f j8 -j21 r
11m -16m l a 30 - m 14r j 22p j3 yu 4 pl
17m -19m g m15- m 21v yy 4 l yy 16 yy 16 la
20m-23m 22m-31l ww 1617 a
24m-31m b j1-j7 n yy 18 r
h j8 no
3 YEARS

O 22 -O 28 Å O 29 PS N 9 N -18 S X
O 29 S N 18 B
O 30 B -N 5
N 678 T -N 8 TOS 10 M ML 23 N MM

The expert assumed that B was for Bergen, S Stavanger, O Oslo, L London, R Rome, P Paris, M stood for March, A for April, etc. MM, JJ and ML were initially incomprehensible.

A check of the alien forms and airlines passenger lists against the notes 20 M 23 M marked with O led to the discovery of a Genevieve Lancier who had arrived in Oslo by plane from Geneva on March 20 and stayed in Bergen from March 24-31. The two lines in front indicated that she was in London from March 11-15 and in Geneva from March 16-19, before going to Oslo.

In a short period of time Seland and Berger, with the help of writing experts and their own imagination, succeeded in finding her route to Bergen. Additionally, they connected her to Claudia Tielt who, according to the passenger list, had traveled from Bergen at 08:00 on the April 1 with the speedboat h/b Vingtor to Stavanger and further out of the country to Basel in Switzerland. All of this according to the ticket archive at the express bus central station in Stavanger.

Two foreign check forms from hotels in Bergen showed that Claudia Tielt had stayed at the Bristol hotel on March 25 and at Skandia Hotel until April 1. Her birth date was listed as July 11, 1943 and 1945 respectively.

The investigators were astonished that the woman's identities had already reached the staggering figure of six.
– "My problem at the moment, is the damn boat that should have been taken off shore by the boat association", said Seland in frustration. He had his head full of new confusing information, while at the back of his mind he thought about Henriksen's remarkable behavior when he was informed about the investigation of the crime scene. They knew each other quite well, and it seemed that he did not mean what he said.
"Boat? Is there anything concerning a boat, as well?", Berger looked at Seland, amazed. Seland looked up, clearly thinking about something else and did not reply.

Kripos's written laboratory studies in the case were a laborious work. There were four alien check forms from hotels, three copies of receipts for food, the writing pad that was decoded and a road map for central Norway from Cappelen publishers with descriptions of Geilo, Ustaoset, Finse and Myrdal and details about elevations in the terrain.

No discrepancies of importance were found by comparing the writing. Two of the alien forms were filled out about seven months before the other two. Three of them were filled out with fiber pens and one with a ball pen. This last, from Leenhouwfr in Hordaheimen on November 19, had somewhat of a more irregular left-handed writing and variation in font size and the angle of the pen against the paper. Among other things, the nationality was written as "BELGIE". The first three were similar in design, but seemed to be written by a person with good writing skills. The laboratory concluded as follows:

"The writer in question is probably born and raised in a country other than Norway, and may have had other school norms than those that are common here.

Circumstances related to the writing that may seem individual to the person writing, in accordance with Norwegian standards, may be more general for people in the country from which the writer originates. However, it appears that the writing on the forms is characterized by different individual hallmarks that are characteristic of the person, and can be found correspondingly in the different pieces of writing. Part of these characteristic agreements I have highlighted in red on photographs in attached folder II with enlargements of the handwriting. In my opinion - the conformities are so extensive that it seems difficult to explain them as merely random, and that they must be a strong indication that there is one identity only".

He further concluded that the last form had the same characteristic features as the other ones, but it seemed that the person who wrote, intentionally tried to make the handwriting unrecognizable.

Elements emphasized were the overall impression of the signature, placement of the writing in the line, the punctuation, and special formatting of letters and numbers. For example, the indentation, the oval shapes and heights of the letter a and d, the form of the letter g and G, the pole and loop in the letter k, the star design of r and R, s and ss, as well as the method of writing and the design of numbers. The conclusion was, respectively, that "there is a high probability that the person who performed the writing is the same".

The atmosphere at the investigation headquarters, as in the rest of the city, was clearly tense and in addition marked by a certain frustrated excitement. The overwhelming information about all of the identities eventually made sure that the case achieved international interest.

Seland, who had just received the day's press report, was both frustrated and slightly jealous of leaders and agents in the department who failed to stay silent and had shown their faces to the press. The day before the newspapers had been full of rumors that the woman supposedly was an Israeli and probably a secret agent. The newest edition of the local newspaper, quoted the police denying the rumors, which resulted in the following headline:

"The woman has an American name. It is unknown to us whether she is from Israel."

- "Even our own people cannot shut up!" exclaimed Seland. – "This means that we get a lot of shit and extra work explaining to the US ambassador and the other "Yankees" that we have no basis for such assumptions. And for God's sake, don't even get me started with Mossad and the rest of the Middle East bullshit! Embarrassing! Especially when it could even prove to be right".

Seland calmed down and leaned back in the chair with a serious expression. Berger had compassionately and with some discomfort followed Seland's outbreak and wanted to get the discussion onto a different track. With a thoughtful expression on his face, he secretly shoved the other local newspaper with the heading "Israeli deserter?" under the office desk,

"This is a case for our own fellow officers in the drug department, there is no doubt
out it! All those trips and all the names suggest a lot of money and drugs." Berger was
ack in the office chair and looked carefully at Seland. He felt a hint of powerlessness
nd needed to take control of the situation. - "Typical drug threat. She must have been
o ridiculously scared that suicide was the only way out!" he continued.

Seland sipped his cold coffee. - "Well, that's a possibility, but both our own people
nd the telex from Interpol in Paris exclude that. In addition, it simply seems too stupid
o spend so much money and impress all that secrecy to sell drugs to the small and
nsignificant market in our sad, Norwegian coastal cities". He spun around in the office
hair. - "No, I think POT knows more than they are telling us. This must be huge. Just
hink of all the fake passports. Just getting them made requires at least one spy
rganization like the KGB. No small entity like drug syndicates can be that
rofessional!"

Berger stared at Seland. They both sat lost in thought for a moment before Berger
icked up the receiver as the phone rang. He diligently took notes and then hung up.
"We were right. The code TOS stand for Trondheim-Oslo-Stavanger as we assumed.
ripos has confirmed that a Claudia Nielsen from Brussels stayed at K.N.A in Stavanger
om October 29-30, before travelling to hotel Neptune in Bergen, where she entered the
ame day as Alexie Zarna-Merchez and moved on to Trondheim with Braathen Safe on
ovember 6 as fraulein Velding. Alien forms from Neptune and Hordaheimen in Bergen
how that Leenhouwfr and Merchez wrote date of birth November 27, but with different
ears - 1943 and 1945. The writing experts have checked flights and hotel remarks and
onfirm that it is the same woman we have followed via Vera Jarle at the Bristol hotel in
rondheim to Stavanger and Bergen.

He flew up from the office chair and shouted, - "She has just been traveling in
ircles!" Seland looked bothered and undoubtedly felt that the case was beginning to
evelop in a disturbing manner. – "What the hell would she do that for"? He asked
rithout aiming the question at anyone in particular. – "I think she may have been
cared or threatened and simply running away from something". He replied to his own
uestion, before counting on his fingers the number of identities they had managed to
race. It was now up to nine. He cried out shaking his head, – "Fuck, this case is just
nbelievable!"

"Well, at least we are dealing with a professional", replied Berger. – "And the safest
ad on the identity is from that chambermaid who heard the woman shouting 'Ich
omme bald' ('I am coming soon') to the German who stayed across the hall. And Basel
n Switzerland, which was the destination of the ticket she bought in Stavanger, is called
ne city with the German heart. She must have been German!" He hit the table
riumphantly with his palms and was clearly pleased with himself.

Along with Berger, he had already concluded that the last known point of
eference for the woman's movements, before she was found, must have been Hotel
Iordaheimen where she stayed on the fourth floor. Several of the staff at the hotel
ecognized the description and had specifically noticed the unique woman. Two of them
hought she had left the hotel once between nine o'clock and twelve o'clock in the
norning on November 13. One of them believed that the woman had talked on the
hone and that she first left the hotel just to return a short while later. The police had
lso shown the drawing of the woman to all the shopkeepers near the hotel. The bank
nanager of the local branch did not exclude the possibility that the woman could have

been there the same morning. In addition, the security officer at the reception seemed t
remember her being picked up by a taxi and he recalled the two suitcases.

The questioning of the taxi drivers who were likely to have driven the woman t
the train station from Hordaheimen Hotel on the morning of the 23, were tiring and
new dead-end. Henriksen and three other officers were forced to give up after about te
of the drivers were questioned, some of them several times, as even though they drov
their taxis near the hotel, not one of them could remember the woman or remembe
even having made the trip.

- "Either taxi drivers are dumber than most people", he thought with himself, - "or the
just shut up to avoid being further involved. Anyway, some may know more than the
care to share".

- "Well, it is nothing new that people tend to shut up as soon they realize we are reall
interested!" "Livredd" ('scared to death') is the word that describes this in Norwegian!

– "The guys who had their taxi's by the Nykirken church that morning may remembe
something if they get some more time", said one of the officers. - "All right, but I don'
really believe that there will be any useful information coming from there", Henrikse
shook his head and closed the witness examination records.

Unfortunately, he was proven right. It was still a riddle how the deceased ha
reached the railway station with two heavy suitcases and from there to Isdalen valley.

One of the first steps that had been taken in the investigation was the review an
cataloging of the contents of the two suitcases. Berger and Henriksen had been a natur
choice for this job.

The suitcases had been sealed at the railway station before being brought into th
police station. Because the offices for the civil servants were small and overfilled by ne
and old documents, Berger and Henriksen could use the cafeteria to sort out th
contents. The other officials paid close attention and constantly peeked through th
swinging door. This probably meant that Berger felt a greater responsibility to mak
sure that the review was done properly.

- "We list shoes and clothes first and then the other items. I'll read and describe it if you
since you are better at writing. If something has been removed or sent for investigatior
we will note it down at the end. Ok?" Henriksen concluded without waiting for a
answer.

Berger nodded towards one of the lunch tables and grabbed the bigger suitcase,
dark brown one without a tag or a brand. They started going through shoes and clothin
first. The list became comprehensive and an example of good old-fashioned police work

SHOES

1 pair of dark brown leather sports shoes, slightly used, unlined, "storm rim" o
the outside leather, wide brown fabric laces, dark rubber footing molded in one
piece, low heel, parallel grooves around the edge of the footing, rough midsection
7 round spots, light brown inner footing with external footwear support. Th
footing is labeled "Marke Salamander". Size number missing.

1 pair of boots, beige, soft suede leather, high shaft, black inner zipper labele
"Éclair". Inside sheep's fur lining, synthetic rubber footing with grooves molde
in one-piece, low heel. Brand and size are cut away with many incisions on bot
boots. Somewhat worn.

1 pair of leather walking shoes, dark violet, half-heeled, 3 cm wide ankle strap with nickel-plated buckle. Sole with grooves in black synthetic material, labeled 6 or 9 under the front of the foot, lined with yellow fabric, worn gold letters inside the heel area, "Bequem" is readable. The shoes were in a plastic bag labeled Nicolsho's Nicolbaby Roma, Via Barberini 30. Phone: 480.869.

"We will certainly be able to trace these", exclaimed Berger. - "The Embassy can help us". Another empty brown bag was labeled "Osc. Rørtvedt Skotøiforretning", Nygaten 8, Stavanger.

"I bet that is where she bought the Viking boots she used in the Isdalen valley! She came here from Stavanger, you know", he nodded to Henriksen. They continued with 1 pair of shoes for indoor usage, leather, navy blue, wedge heel, rubber sole, brand name worn out, "Italy" is readable, size unknown. Lay in unlabeled transparent plastic bag.

Henriksen described the objects and Berger took notes, and the list was longer.

CLOTHING
A. Morning dress, light, wide, flannel, button-fly, 6 blank buttons, without collar, half-length sleeves, strip and flower-patterned ribbon. Factory and size labels have been removed.
B. Tight fitting floral wool dress, half-length sleeves, belt, factory labels removed.
C. Short skirt made of artificial fiber, funnel shaped, woven flower pattern, glossy zipper, hook, no label tag.
D. Green / blue fluffy wool knit sweater with an open neck, no label tag.
E. Navy blue thin wool knitted sweater with high collar, lower part in waistband style, "7 straight and 4 inside out". Factory label cut off, but readable: "48".
F. Thinly knitted, pink cotton sweater, short sleeves, round neck.
G. Thin light blue sweater, fiber, sleeve, round neck, no label tag.
H. Nylon blouse, zigzag pattern violet, pink, green, round neck, factory label cut away.
I. Dark blue nylon undergarment, laces up, down and over the bust, thin braces, no label tag.
J. Dark blue bust holder, laces in cups and front, inner part reinforced at the bottom, 3 spears sewn in, rosette in blue and white between the cups, no label tag.

"Fuck, this is rather shitty!" Henriksen exclaimed as he sat with a pair of long nylon stockings in his hands. - "To sit here and fumble through the most intimate parts of a dead woman's clothes. Can we swap for a while?" He looked at Berger with a somewhat suffering expression. - "Yes, sure! A job is a job", said Berger and took over the description:

K. Dark blue nylon bust holder, thin inner lining, 2 in-sewn braces and uplift-braces under the cups, loop between cups, adjustable shoulder straps with lace ribbons, double loop button system, no label tag.
L. Dark blue panties with laces, lined in the crotch, elastic band around the waist, no label tag.

M. Dark blue, square pattern panties, lined in the crotch, no label tag.

N. Light green nylon panties, elastic band around the waist and thighs, factory label removed.

The list continued with belts, stockings, a black fur coat and various gloves, a pair with a washed out label from "Gant Nyeret Paris 7".

Berger exhailed. - "That was the first. Let's take the second right away, then we're done with this. You're right! It is not exactly a pleasure to fumble around in dead peoples' private things. Especially not a woman's"!

He started describing the contents of the second suitcase:

A. Trench coat, light-colored, 2 hidden pockets, fox leather collars. Labels missing.

B. Leather cap, Cossack-shape, beige, brand label not present.

C. Turquoise coarse crochet hat. No label tag.

D. Mahogany brown "Napoleonic hairstyle" wig. Labeled "Creation Alexandre de Paris".

The list continued with a knitted jacket, a variety of shawls, hair bands, slippers etc. None of the items had label tags.

Furthermore, 500 marks, 130 Norwegian kronas, and a few Belgian and French coins were found in the larger suitcases. The 500 marks were hidden behind a lining in the suitcase.

In addition to clothes and shoes, other items were registered: oval shaped sunglasses; a sanitary towel; a plastic bag with a crystalline sugar-like brownish substance; soup spoon of steel; a ladie's bag; a small half-full perfume bottle labeled "Jacques Esterel Paris"; a pair of dark round sunglasses; a plastic purse with a label from a bank called "Kjøbmandsbanken"; a laboratory knife branded "INOX 4"; 4 maps from Cappelen publishing and Stuttgart Reise; the route plan for Hurtigruten 1970-71 marked NOK 183, - / 256, - NSB route; a note pad with numbers and letters; a small red book with a photo of Madonna and her child; an English postcard, and a Norwegian postcard with a winter motive. Names and factory labels were largely removed from all of the items.

In the smaller suitcase, washing gloves were also found along with clean cotton, a half a bottle of White Curacau, 6 plastic teaspoons, a fork marked "Hackvan Finland"; 2 plastic drinking glasses made in France labeled Gilac / Pola; an envelope labeled "Hotel Regina Genève Suisse"; a paper label with the imprint "London"; the remains of a candle; Dagbladet for Saturday the September 21, 1970; half of the schedule for Hurtigruten; SAS and Braathen's airline schedules in Norway; a make-up bag; Kleenex paper,;various plastic bottle tubes and containers with labels scraped off; a tube of 250 gram of cortisone cream with a red label reading "Traneapoteket Bergen" (a pharmacy in Bergen) and the name and date scratched away; mascara, lipstick, a tube branded "Baranne France"; matches from "Beate Uhse 239 Flensburg"; matches from "Hotel Nobel, Karl Johansgt. 33 Oslo"; a little round compass; various rings; a pair of sunglasses with broken glass (already sent to the technical department); and a bottle of Tonipan samme.

The two investigators were tired of all the details, but now had a far more nuanced view of the lost woman's background. At the same time they believed that some of the possessions could clearly lead to the solution of the mystery. The cards and the matches were immediately picked out for the first part of the investigation.

All brands were to a large degree systematically removed and scraped away in both of the suitcases. Both Berger and Henriksen were very fascinated with the significant amount of trouble that the woman, or others, had gone through when removing brands to minimize the traces that were left behind. The fact that the woman was found dead, gave no answer whatsoever to the secrecy around her identity.

– "At least this is on a completely different and more professional level than we have been before", Berger said to Henriksen in a serious tone. – "Yes, both the content and the removal of marks. I think it would be smart to get a comment from an outside expert, based on these findings", Kristiansen added in agreement.

Two of the city's prominent clothing retailers were asked to review the clothing and shoes from the two suitcases and give an expert opinion on the qualities and origins of the items. The gentlemen noted that many of the items were not common in Norway. For example, the nylon stockings, intended to dress the entire leg up to the crotch, were not sold in Norway. When asked to share the general impression they got from the woman's clothes and items, they both explained that they were left with an "Italian feeling" and both thought that she had "Italian taste" in clothing and underwear.

The manager of the city's leading shop for items of interest to travelers, confirmed after reviewing the suitcases and their contents, that most of the items were made in Europe and that only a few of them could have been purchased in Norway.

Following these external expert inspections, Berger and Henriksen, felt that they were now more confident in their belief that the woman was not Norwegian. Berger thought that she might have come from southern Germany somewhere whereas Henriksen was inclined towards an Italian origin.

Later that day, Berger went and got a copy of the local newspaper. As usual, the press had obtained new information. – "Ha" He exclaimed aloud as he re-entered the office. - "This time it is obvious that they have no grounds for their statements! Unless, someone took 6500 marks from the suitcase!" Berger said, bursting out in laughter. Henriksen, was equally amused.

The headline said the following:

"The woman from Isdalen valley had a suitcase containing, among other things, 6-7000 German marks and some Norwegian money, which was hidden among the suitcase contents."

Bergen, December 1970

Two weeks after the discovery of the body - the case took a new turn. The investigators in Bergen received very surprising new information through a Norwegian journal, *Kriminaljournalen*. An observant reader called the police office and told them about an article titled *Bomber Over America,* which also showed photographs of the wanted fugitive Katy Wilkinson. The reader had seen the drawing of the dead woman in the daily press and believed it to resemble the image of Wilkinson, described as a terrorist, wanted by the FBI and probably having escaped to Europe. For a long time, the FBI had placed agents, in cooperation with Interpol, strategically in the areas surrounding Bader-Meinhof, without finding any trace of Wilkinson.

The article was quickly obtained and Berger looked at the picture of the woman in the magazine with eyes as big as saucers. - "Damn, seems like we solved the case!"

Just to be sure, he immediately sent the article through the telex to the United States Legal-attaché at the Embassy in Copenhagen with a request asking if this could be the woman from Isdalen valley. The attaché had previously received the wanted notice and two photographs of plastic bottles found at the scene. He had been very cooperative and confirmed having sent them for investigation in New York.

Berger triumphantly entered Seland's office with the article and showed him the picture. - "Do you recognize this lady?" he asked with excitement in his voice.
They examined the big photograph of the woman in the article that Berger held up, next to the drawing from Hetland. - "This is really shaping up", Seland said almost devoutly.

He took the magazine and skimmed quickly through the article. 21 "Black Panthers" were arrested in 1969 when they were planning a bombing on several warehouses in New York. A wave of bomb-threats spread throughout the country - 600 in New York alone. Smaller groups sprung up and, among other incidents, 26 telephone booths were bombarded with Molotov cocktails in Los Angeles. A group of left-wing radicals, including Gold and Wilkinson, were wanted because they produced homemade bombs. Unfortunately, one of these must have been triggered in the basement of Wilkinson's parents' house, on 18 West and 11th street in Greenwich Village. The house was completely blasted and through a large hole in the facade, two women were seen when they crept out and escaped. One was thought to have been Wilkinson. Ted Gold was found dead in the house.

After questioning other survivors, it became evident that the group had intended to use bombs as a terrorist tool to push the University of Columbia to pay the bail for the imprisoned "panthers". The case had huge press coverage, even more so because stars like Jane Fonda and Dustin Hoffman had apartments in the neighboring houses. Even though all police units were in the highest state of preparedness, and airports, roads and railway stations strictly monitored, the arrest of Katy Wilkinson failed. It was believed later that she had escaped abroad, probably to Europe.

– "This can certainly fit well in with our person", Seland nodded after a while. – "We should talk to POT to hear what they think".

– "I have already sent a copy to "Legal" at the US Embassy in Copenhagen", Berger replied. – "He will probably contact us soon with some answers, as usual".

The Police in Bergen had sent several requests to the FBI and the US Embassy in Copenhagen in order to answer whether any Americans could have been on flights to or from Bergen or staying at hotels in Bergen simultaneously with the deceased woman. The answers came back quickly, but none of them had given any new clues, as they generally described only ordinary business people with decent alibies for their visits and without criminal records.

But oddly enough, Berger received no answer from the US Embassy in openhagen this time. They had always been extremely helpful and prompt in their answers. Instead, Seland received a report, with a copy of a short note from POT to ripos, one week later. The note stated that there was no wanted notice for the woman : Interpol. Furthermore, it contained a clear request to not carry out further investigations about Wilkinson, either in Europe or by inquires to the United States. The ase was suspended. The disappointment was enormous at the offices in Bergen. "How in God's name can we do a good job when we have our hands and feet bound?" eland murmured and cursed. - "Everybody knows that we will be held responsible, no latter when the results are measured"!

he message from the CIA at that time, to Interpol in Paris and on to POT in Norway, ad been categorical and ambiguous. The three investigators in the Surveillance Center ocated in Oslo, were rather surprised when they read the following message:

"The Wilkinson case is not to be pursued in any way".

he announcement was signed by Commander Jeff Conahan, Head of the European livision and countersigned by the Paris leading division of Interpol in Paris. The lessage put an immediate stop to all further investigation on this path.

Thousands of investigators and several assistants in Bergen were now working round the clock on the case, both day and night. Most people were highly committed nd keen, not least because of the special nature of the case, and that it was so different om anything an ordinary provincial policeman could expect to experience at work. It as particularly exciting for many investigators who were put on the case from other epartments such as "Order and Theft-Injury". Now they got to experience "real" police ork with the murder investigators from the crime department.

eland shook his head over superficial crime department aspirants, but was still pleased ith all the information they provided. He smiled, but had to laugh aloud when he howed Berger the report from one who had been on the scene with a mine detector and oncluded the following:

"The writer of the report investigated the crime scene himself with a magnet!"

he contact with the major international secret service – the organizations, the press ttention and the feeling of having the responsibility of such a big case, meant that most eople did their job far beyond what they normally would have done.

Hundreds of interviews and follow-ups were constantly reported and reviewed. Ine of the problems with such a way of working was that a lot of tips and calls were uled by fear, envy and ignorance. Many called about a suspicious neighbor or people hey knew who would have stated something strange or behaved "abnormally". Iowever, everything was taken seriously and followed up by police investigators, with ritten reports for later consideration.

Determining the time of death in order to be more certain about following the ight leads and sort out the most interesting witnesses became a hard nut to crack in the investigation and Seland concentrated on the testimonies gathered between Novembe 22-24. He had a feeling they were now approaching a solution in this case.

He decided to gather the most interesting explanations and put them int context. One lady said that on November 23, at about midnight while she was driving o her way to Bergen, she had seen a big dirty car. The car had two women in the fron made a stop close to Isdalen valley and one of them went out of the car. She looked lik the drawing in the newspapers, had dark hair in a ponytail, fastened at the neck and leather coat with leather trimmings. She had pretty features and looked like she wa born outside of Norway.

On November 22, a man went on a Sunday trip with his wife pas Svartediksvannet Lake in Isdalen valley and up the hills in the north. They looked ove at Dødsdalen valley and noticed a funnel of smoke, without seeing any people there. Th weather was gray and the smoke dissolved shortly afterwards.

A bus driver remembered driving a woman who could fit the description, on hi route to Isdalen valley. He shouted "Svartediksveien" over the speaker to announce th stop and remembered she pointed up in the air as to ask him before she left the bus This could have been between November 15th and 25th.

A woman believed to have seen the deceased at a painting exhibition at the Ar Society on November 22, around 12:30. She especially remembered the two upper teet she thought were framed with gold. When she was presented with the photo of the teet from the autopsy, she could not tell if they were the same. She didn't recognize th woman she had described from the drawing of the deceased's profile.

A resident in a mountainous area outside Bergen, overlooking the Isdalen valley became aware of a patch of fog when she looked out of her bathroom window aroun midnight. Her first thought was that it came from a bonfire, but she had assumed it wa the forest company burning twigs. She could not verify whether this did indeed occur o November 23.

A young man saw a man and a woman descend towards Dødsdalen valley from the path to Ulrikken Mountain, but they later disappeared. Both wore dark clothes.

On November 21, a woman in her mid twenties stopped a young student an asked for "vino" and was obviously looking for a place to purchase wine. She was abou 165 tall, slim with somewhat wide hips, dark hair with a reddish tint, maxi coat an pants.

On November 19, three friends saw a young lady in Isdalen valley. She seeme "arrogant", 23-30 years, 170 Centimeter tall, seemed to be from the south, her face c brownish color, wearing a jacket and pants and had a shoulder bag. They did not see he again.

A hiker explained that a woman as described in the press walked in front of hin in the Isdalen valley. He passed her, but did not see her again. He later passed a van with two people in the front. Further on, a man in a training suit jogged towards the city The witness could not confirm the exact time other than between November 21 and 29.

A forest worker reported that he had seen a woman with the description i Isdalen valley. He had also seen smoke or fog in Dødsdalen (the Death Valley) o November 23, but added that after many years of observing the special climati conditions and smoke patches in the valley, he had learned to wait and see if it resolve itself before he could know if the smoke was from fire or fog.

A jogger said that he had seen two people in the valley on November 23 and that hey spoke a foreign language. He did not remember any smoke.

An employee of the army, who had Mondays free, went into the valley around 12 m on November 23. He saw vague "smoke" lying like a belt over the trees in the woodland north of the stream in Dødsdalen valley, wondering if it could come from a bonfire, but assumed it was fog.

A firefighter on a control mission had driven into the valley at 11:50 on November 23 and stopped at the quarry. He remembered having seen a man between 30 and 40 years old on the way out of the valley. He had not noticed any smoke in the gray weather.

A cyclist who knew that he was in the valley on Monday at 12 o'clock said that for a minute he had stood and looked at a funnel of smoke in front of Dødsdalen valley before it dissolved so he had assumed it was fog.

By the end of the week most investigators were pretty run down. In addition to the most relevant statements, investigators and interrogators had worked through hundreds of uninteresting inquiries.

Seland, Berger and three others had gathered and read all the reports of importance and needed a break for the summary and conclusion. Seland gave Berger thumbs up. - "Tell the people that we will take an extra meeting this afternoon, around 2 o'clock. We should keep the chief of police and lawyers out of it. Use the cafeteria on the fourth floor, the other rooms are too small".

Because of the immense pressure and the experience of brotherhood, it almost seemed like everybody was entitled to a break, and most of the police officers were having coffee and rolling cigarettes when Seland entered with a stack of papers. He sat down at the table that was rigged up near the sandwich sales counter. – "What we must determine now is the time of death and how to figure out the identity of this female". He looked at Berger who continued, – "We are sure that she left the hotel Hordaheimen in a taxi at approximately 10:30 am on Monday, November 23. Then all tracks disappear until she is found dead on Sunday, November 29 in the valley of Dødsdalen. The pathologist thinks that somewhere between November 23 and 26 is the correct date of death, probably closer to the 26. And we have no information about possible places of residence after Monday. He looked at the assembly. - "Suggestions?"

A hand went up and one of the officers who had gone from house to house at the entrance to Isdalen valley and questioned the residents began to talk. – "The issue with the smoke cloud starts to become quite concrete. We have the testimony of the woman who saw smoke from their home on the mountainside on November 13; then there is the forest worker and not least the cyclist and even more. And we have many who say they have passed a woman similar to the description in the newspaper, during their trip to the valley that day. No other moments in time during that week have so many observations. As we see in our group, it is most likely that she died on Monday, November 23. He sat down and there was a lot of discussion and turmoil until another officer's arm went up.

– "We did a test on the issue with the smoke. The report is with Berger. We brought dogs and checked the whole area around the scene. It seemed as if the fog from the forest north of the scene gathered into fog flakes as soon as it emerged in the clearing and rose like a pillar of smoke before it evaporated. Two men did a test from the north

side of the water and the road, but the strange thing is that there was nothing to see. In my opinion, it's likely that if someone has seen smoke from that side that it was hardly common fog!"
- "Agreed", Seland replied. "Everything indicates that November 23 is the correct date. As for who she was, the best we can come up with is that the girl on Neptune heard her speak German, and that he, the youth, - that I think talked to her - heard the question 'vino?'"

One of the younger investigators had gone to every single house in Isdalen valley to question the villagers, now raised his arm. – "We went through the foreign books from Neptune and Hotel Norway and found that several foreign and Norwegian officers from the nuclear energy institute at Kjeller, outside Oslo, had arrived as representatives of NATO. They were supposedly on their way to Haakonsvern. In the days before our lady arrived at Neptune as Alexia Zarna Merchez, two Russians stayed there. All this was between the October 30 and November 5. The Germans at Neptune claimed that they had a repair job at Mjellemverftet on Laksevåg and the rest were marines attending a course at Haakonsvern.

At the hotel Rosenkranz, a German and a Swiss stayed in the same hallway vis-a-vis the woman's room, and similarly on the floor above. At least there were plenty of foreigners in town, and I think she had something to do with them. She did not speak Norwegian at all. By the way, in the interrogation of the hotels and from several of the people who were questioned about Isdalen we have heard that they had seen a man as well, for example the jogger. The man may well have been a foreigner, right"? He looked inquiringly for support from Henriksen.
- "Okay", Seland said, as he began to feel that the discussion had started to take an unwanted direction. - "I think we'll finish there. We conclude with November 23 and that she is probably Southern European. We must go through all the hotels again and see if we find more. Berger or I will travel to Trondheim and check there. Kripos has announced that the intelligence service could question the Germans, who can be contacted, from the hotel".

He continued and sneered at his last comment before he thanked everyone and ended the meeting. - "Berger and I will forget about Paris and Geneva this time around! Thank you for your attendance and nice work so far guys!"

Seland gazed thoughtfully out the window onto a large construction crane at work and sighed heavily as he remembered that the community effort of getting the boat ashore was planned this week.

Bergen, December 1970

Seland almost dived in the door of the "chamber" as the police station in Bergen was called among the local people. The weather was at its worst with southwestern storm gusts, sleet and rain. He shook his coat and threw a wet hat down on the guest chair before rushing over to the coffee machine, rubbing his freezing blue hands around the hot coffee pot.
- "Something new today"? He asked as he poured himself a cup of coffee and turned to Berger, who was staring out the window at the storm. - "The sheriff in Geilo sent a telex that the director at Bergsjø Tourist Hotel earlier this autumn was asked on the

telephone by a foreign lady who asked Lorc if two single rooms had to be pre-booked or if one could only stay at the hotel without booking in advance. He noted down the request". Berger waved with his arm. - "It is weird, however, that we received a new message from Kripos, who has considered this, telling us that the directors daughter claims the request did not come this year, but last year and concerned a booking long time in advance. Have you ever heard bullshit like that before?" Berger continued. – "We have also received a report from the sheriff in Oppdal about an Italian traveling with a lady. Pretty interesting! By the way, we should go to Trondheim soon and check the lead on the hotels up there". He looked inquiringly at Seland.

– "And then it was the issue with Paris and Geneva too, but when they tell us that there is no money, it's hopeless. By the way, I do not like the so-called "help" we receive from the Ministry of Justice and Kripos or POT for that matter". Berger folded his arms over his chest and looked sharply at Seland.

For a minute Seland looked like he would agree but picked up the report from the sheriff in Oppdal and sat down to read it through. As he read, he uttered things like "Jesus!" and "What?"

The sheriff in Oppdal had received the wanted notice with the drawing of the deceased. At the small ski resort in Oppdal it was noticed when different-looking tourists moved around outside the tourist season. A woman, similar to the one in the drawing, except that she had a somewhat flatter nose, had arrived in Oppdal by train from Stockholm via Oslo, apparently alone. An Italian artist from Milan who traveled around Norway and collected motives for postcards, had met her randomly at the square in Oppdal. She had little money and Tromboli, as he was called, invited her to dinner with some friends he had from several previous visits in Norway. During the dinner, she had told him that she was from South Africa, from a small town north of Johannesburg, and that she earned well enough to travel half a year to see beautiful places. She had no other reason to visit Norway.

The Oppdal Tourist Hotel had not filled out an alien form on the woman nor did they have anything that was suited to use for text sample analysis. She had left Oppdal together with the Italian on October 3, after having stayed for one night, without revealing her name. Tromboli had told his friends that he had taken a car from Stockholm across Storlien to Trondheim. They seemed to remember that the girl was called Lorett Junkin. Seland put the report on Berger's desk. - "Hmm, we must follow up on this. We should compare them to the letters on the postcard right away. Contact Kripos and have them track the Italian for questioning. If he has left Norway, Interpol must do a house search at his home in Milan".

He sat down and wrote a request describing Tromboli to police forces nationwide and sent it as soon as it was ready. Within a few hours, he received a response from Kristiansand, stated that they had a police report that had been dismissed for the requested person. Seland felt his pulse rise when he read the message.

Kripos was informed immediately and replied that neither the Italian nor the woman could be found in Norway, but that the embassy in Rome was to send a search party to Tromboli's house. Kripos also sent notice that they wanted to follow this lead. - "Hair-raising! No fucking way! Send inexperienced amateur ambassadors to follow up on such a lead! It is never going to happen!" He curled up the letter and threw it into the trash bin.

Seland was understandably angry and cursed after the recent development. With Kripos' constant involvement, the heavy workload of reports to be reviewed and considered hanging over him, it was not a good time for him to travel to Trondheim to get testimonies from service staff at the Bristol hotel. However, the police chief had ordered him to travel, as he was his most experienced man. Kripos had announced that the woman's itinerary and stay were to be investigated and described in detail and at the same time made it clear that this was a job for investigative management. Seland thought it was more than all right to be in the "most experienced" category according to the police chief, but what annoyed him was that tomorrow was his day off and he had planned to do some community work for the boat association. Now, it appeared he had to pay them, to get off the hook.

The association had a harbor near the naval base in Haakonsvern. He had therefore immediately associated the base with the events of yesterday's joint meeting when one of the officers spoke about the people from NATO and the foreigners at the hotel.

– "If she has had anything to do with any of those people, it's likely that she has something to do with espionage", he thought to himself. But when he thought about all the hundreds of times he had passed the base by boat, it seemed excessively dramatic and unlikely. – "We should probably keep it as a backup theory", he muttered to himself as he stared at the newspaper articles that were glued up over the wall in front of the desk.

He grabbed the phone and called Svein Johannesen at the police department in Trondheim. Johannessen was pleasantly surprised and enthusiastic and they had a lengthy conversation on the phone about the case in Bergen. They also shared memories about their time at the police academy and in Sweden during the war. Before saying goodbye they agreed that Johannessen would on a pick Seland up at his hotel in Trondheim the following day. There was already a room booked at the Bristol hotel, the same room that "Vera Jarle" had stayed in.

The routine police work had just begun, such as the examination of the hotel and retrieving information from the restaurant staff. Officers Henriksen and Berger had distributed the tasks between the investigators and coordinated and processed the information contained in the reports.

Already on December 3, the police had contacted the Trane pharmacy in Bergen, from where the cortisone cream, found in the woman's suitcase, had been purchased. Berger decided to interview every employee at the pharmacy, including the owners. He had a good feeling that they would find decisive evidence of the woman's true identity. The pharmacy must have had a doctor's approval or at least an approved prescription from elsewhere to be able to deliver the ointment. - "With a little luck", Berger thought, "we will find the person who was reimbursed the expenses for the ointment from the Social Security Fund"!

Although the date and the doctor's name were scraped away, he thought it should clearly be possible to trace the handwriting. Pharmacist Lippke with his kind appearance, was about 55 years old, bald and had large round "pharmacy glasses". He was an exceptionally nice and helpful man.

Lippke believed that the label had been filled out as usual, with name, date and the doctor's instructions for usage. Typically, prescriptions were for one time only, but

1 some cases for one year at a time. The pharmacist assumed it was a one-time
rescription, but could not make sense of the doctor's handwriting or the personal mark
f the pharmacy employee who had issued the ointment. In some cases, a pharmacy
ould be able to deliver ointment several times on a regular prescription, but according
) Lippke, this was a question of discretion and never occurred at his pharmacy. The
riting could resemble either Dr. Sander or Bengtson, but none of them remembered
nything about writing the prescription, or the unknown woman. Dr. Sander said that
he usually used the same text, "on the skin, thin layer, 2-3 times daily". Both said they
rescribed the ointment quite often, and the pharmacist believed that the pharmacy
ssued about 20 such daily. Lippke wanted to confirm this with the other employees but
oncluded that there was no possibility that the pharmacy could in any way trace the
atient's identity. Berger cursed both the sloppy physician's writing and pharmacists.
ust as he left the pharmacy, Lippke said, - "By the way, I told your colleague the same
hing the first time you were here, it's impossible to recognize that handwriting".
erger could not help but to show his surprise, - "What are you saying, has someone
een here before, asking questions?"- "Yes, a blond guy, who first had the prescription",
he pharmacist replied. - "Oh yes, right", Berger kept his cool and hid how frustrated he
vas before he thanked them for the information and left the pharmacy.

He informed Seland about the matter as soon as he returned to the office. As
erger expected Seland was pissed. - "To hell with both POT and Kripos, they must be
he ones that let the guy check the prescription from the suitcase right away. Anyway, I'll
ive him hell for this so he never needs to doubt that he has to go through the official
hannels in this department! What worries me is that when someone has the audacity to
ake important evidence in that way, it must solely be due to an order from a superior.
n addition, we will need to insist on improving the routines on technical so that they do
ot give anyone access to such material. It's fucked up that the guy has taken out
mportant material and then put it back again without notifying us! What else might
ave been taken when the security is that shitty? And if the POT is behind this, we must
e aware of their involvement in the further investigation as well. As if we do not have
nough to worry about already!"

Seland cursed and started to flip through the letters on the desk. As soon as
erger had left, he went to the chief of police's office with a tiny feeling of malicious
leasure and reported what had happened.

he response from the chief of the Social Security Fund later that week showed that no
efunds were paid for cortisone cream in the last six months. Seland waved his arms and
tarted to swear continuously.

The chief of police, who by the way had not engaged in the case, shrugged his
houlders and mumbled something like - "as expected".

Police officer Henriksen was quite excited after hearing from the director at the
Jeptune Hotel that one of the chamber maids remembered the woman well and had
omething to say. As he himself had been among the people who had found the woman
nd later participated in the crime scene investigation, he thought the best solution
vould be to handle this interview himself.

As both of them had seen and formed their own opinions of the woman, he
imself after her death and the maid before, it could be interesting to see the
onclusions set against each other, Henriksen thought to himself.

In the time after the inspection of the crime scene and the conclusion of suicide an ever-increasing doubt had arisen about the conclusions they had made and whether they were right. He did not believe that everything was so simple. These were the conclusions he had reached on his own:

> The woman had not been sufficiently affected by pills or alcohol that it could have resulted in her losing control of herself. The Fenemal pills were very weak and made to be soluble over time! They were no sleeping pills, as the first report indicated. They were only meant to have a calming effect. Especially unsuitable for suicide in any case!

He was thinking about Judy Garland, the movie star, and her misuse of pills. He had read about it in his wife Else's weekly woman's magazine. - "She really looks like Garland," he had told Else one morning. - "We should not ignore the fact that nerves play a part here as well."
- "You can talk about death and so forth", Elsa replied, "but not in front of the kids at the breakfast table!" He had quickly "come down to earth" again after letting himself get too involved in the matter.

Back at the office, the riddle continued. He concluded that she would hardly have tried to kill herself by using a few weak tranquilizing pills, far out in a cold, wet and unknown mountain range! Henriksen was caught in a stream of thoughts. Half a bottle of liqueur meant almost nothing in this context. A note from Kripos confirmed that the alcohol level was only 0.2 to 0.3. The container that might have had some clean petrol which was not even empty or exploded, could hardly give off the severe heat development that was observed. The cold weather and the deserted location were a highly unlikely setting for a suicide. Besides, she probably had not worn her boots then. And the fact that her watch was taken off the wrist as the chain was burned on the inside! That the watch had stopped at 12:30 seemed meaningless in a suicide scenario. And of course, the fact that there were so many identities and that the brand labels that had been removed, made him doubt. In addition, he was of the understanding that was shared by most other investigators, that carbon poisoning in open air was not possible!
- "And specially not from a normal bonfire", he said out loud. Deeply involved in his own thought, Henriksen went up the stairs to hotel Neptune and into the reception to meet the chambermaid.

Trondheim - Bergen, December 1970

Police officer Svein Johannesen stood in the arrivals hall and searched for Seland among the group of passengers that had landed on the first SAS morning flight from Bergen via Ålesund, that day. Although it was 25-30 years since the last time they had met, he expected to recognize Seland at sight. And surely, vice versa. In fact, he knew little about the matter from Bergen, but knew that POT and Kripos had worked significantly on the matter as well.

When Seland came around the corner, they simultaneously recognized each other and smiled and waved. Just like identical twins they smiled equally wide and patted ach other warmly on their shoulders. They felt the roots of their friendship from days ong gone.

Johannesen guided his guest to the brand new Volvo Amazon, which was the rondheim police's newly earned pride. On the way in from Værnes the conversations vas lively.

- "There's one thing in this case I've wondered a bit about", Johannesen looked at ieland with an important smile, "The chief of POT, Bruun, has probably not mentioned o you that we had a little strange coincidence happening while the lady was here?" ieland hesitated a little, - "No, I cannot recall that". He looked curiously at Johannesen.

"Do you think she traveled through Oslo"? Seland still did not understand what ohannesen was referring to.

- "No, on the same day this Jarla landed, one of the top chiefs of Russian intelligence in Jorway, came to Trondheim! The amazing thing is that he landed just ten minutes after ter so that if there was a connection, they even had time to talk to each other at the irport!"

"Is it even fucking possible?" Seland stared at Johannesen. "POT - Bruun cannot just void telling us if they knew"?

- "Well, for some reason, he must have", replied Johannesen. – "A friend of mine in 'OT mentioned that they did not expect that the guy had been here. The Ministry had tot received a travel inquiry and Bruun's team had not received a travel inquiry or toticed that he had left Oslo", Johannesen added.

- "Embarrassing if you ask me", replied Seland. Johannesen nodded.

- "Probably there is more to this case than we "simple workers" will ever know. I felt I hould tell you that in any case".

Seland thought about the new piece of information as they approached the city. Jnlike most cases in the past, this one became more unreal and incomprehensible the nore they found out.

They agreed to meet at the Bristol hotel, the following morning after Seland had become a little more familiar with the place and spent the day forming an opinion on low the woman had behaved when she was in Trondheim.

Ie got room number 427, the same as the lady had when she was there, and thought it vas a little strange and unreal. With the information about the woman in mind, he miffed the air after the somewhat special perfume that several of the people that had been questioned had noticed. For a moment, he almost seemed to smell a slight scent, as t memory of something sensual and female and realized that she had obviously had tyle and elegance. But far behind in the subconscious "a bell rang" and reminded him hat all matters were equally important to a policeman.

- "Well", he grinned, "it wouldn't harm anybody to spend some time on high-status vork".

The next morning Seland, Johannesen and an officer from the foreign police, went hrough the alien forms from November. They did not find anything new and decided to ook closer at what Johannesen already had about Vera Jarle. She had stayed at Bristol rom November 6-9 and had listed Antwerp her birthplace on the form. They decided to heck banks and travel agencies nearby.

The Fellesbanken bank, the hotel and Braathen ticket office all said that they had received 100 German marks from the Braathen Safe. The only one that had bought tickets was a person called I. She traveled by airport express bus at 12:15 and had a ticket to Oslo with bus number 255 at 13:20. From there she had a ticket to Stavanger bus number 203 with an arrival at 16:45. Nobody at the Braathen office remembered the person responsible for the order. The bank clerks could not remember the woman either.

One of the porters at Bristol remembered the woman well. He described her as medium to tall, dark hair, brown eyes, about 30 years old, and wearing dark clothes. He remembered that the bill was 138 kroners when she left, and after seeing the photos Seland had from the suitcases of the deceased, he confirmed that he recognized the darkest one.

The waiter's testimony confirmed that they were on the right track. By 19:30 the woman had entered the dining room on the second floor and one of the waiters had helped her translate the dinner menu that was in Norwegian. She had ordered halibut, that the waiter had called "hellebarde" in English. He asked if she was English but got the answer "Belgian". He then told her that the football team Standard Liege had just visited Trondheim, and she replied that she had been in Liege. He had taken the time to study her and remembered that her face was somehow oval, but her cheekbones were high, without her having an Asian appearance.

The chambermaid described the woman with brown and reddish modern hair, a pretty face and about 25-30 years old. She could not remember that she had dark hair as the doorman had said. When Seland showed her the photo of the suitcase she exclaimed, - "There is the suitcase!" She said without doubt that the dark brown, extra wide suitcase was the same as she had seen in room 427 and that had belonged to the lady. She also said that while cleaning the room she had noticed a strong smell of perfume, not uncomfortable, and that the lady had had a lot of bottles and vials on the mirror shelf. She often went out and left for half an hour or an hour at the time. She always locked the room door, even though she was just going to the common room across the hall.

Another of the porters described the woman as "shortly put: a pretty lady". He remembered her with dark hair, brown eyes, long trousers and dark clothes. He had even carried her two suitcases into the elevator and immediately recognized them in the photo Seland had, both the dark one and the smaller light one.

Seland eventually felt that there was no more to gain by staying longer in Trondheim. He confirmed that the former theory concerning Jarle and Selling had to be correct. Back in Bergen, they should take a close look at the reports from Stavanger and see if anything else could be found there. The only thing that really bothered him, and he would ask POT about it later, was why he had not received the information that the KGB agent had been there at the same time as she was.

Two days after the visit and after Seland had sent his report to Kripos, Johannesen was called in by a furious leader at POT, who wanted to know what reasons and rights he had to comment on internal intelligence cases to random local police officers. There was no doubt that Bruun felt deceived and had not been up to date with the situation.

Johannesen showed his own report sent to both POT and Kripos and where the Russian visitor from the embassy, Mr. Lenktov, was registered at the airport in the standard manner. Likewise, that he returned to Oslo the same day.

While Seland was in Trondheim, Henriksen welcomed the first of the convened hotel staff at Neptune. Throughout the morning he had felt turmoil and an intuitively tingling feeling that he had missed something. Something did not seem right. He was not able to put his finger on it. But he was convinced that something was wrong and did not fit together in his pattern of investigation. And in accordance with his experiences with previous cases, he felt confident that it would sooner or later come to him. It was precisely that assurance that eventually gave him the necessary sense of security that he would do a good job in the profession as a police investigator.

- "Of course! How f foolish of me!" Henriksen jumped up in the armchair and hit his fist in his palm with a bang. The young maid who had been silently waiting to be questioned, looked terrified with huge eyes at the cop who was suddenly back in the real world. – "Sorry, I completely drifted away", he explained to the girl. – "This really has nothing to do with you! Listen can you wait for a moment outside in the hallway? I just need to make a phone call first".

The girl looked relieved and disappeared out the door. Henriksen sat in the chair again and leaned back with his eyes closed while pressing both palms against his temples.

He almost remembered the report from the forensic medical practitioners, word by word, in its entirety. The analysis of the deceased's lungs had been as follows: "Nothing special to notice". At the same time, concerning the conclusion of suicide, they wrote that "traces of soot particles in the trachea" were found.

Of course the conclusion must be wrong! If the woman had sprinkled herself with gasoline to ignite, the lungs would contain significant amounts of vapor from petrol or residues of such.

He even remembered an old book by Agatha Christie, where just this scenario had revealed a murder! When the pathologists only found traces of soot in the trachea, and not steam in the lungs, she would have had to be surprised by a sudden fire and could not have done it herself!!

- "Ha! ", he said as he pounded his head triumphantly back against the wall, liberated by the conclusion that almost tumbled out of his mind. Grinning, he thought about the fact that Seland and Kripos now had to realize that it could not be suicide. How could we have overlooked this? It is as if it was taken from a schoolbook. Thus, only two possibilities remained; the accident scenario and the murder scenario. Henriksen was in high spirits.

– "Concentrate for fuck's sake!" He said to himself. The scenario with the accident was questionable. In addition, the investigative management had already excluded it as a possible cause. Not least because there was no trace of where the woman could have had enough gasoline to bring on an accident that would have given off such a huge explosive fire. Theoretically, it could be argued that the woman, by committing suicide, could have achieved such a fire by first sprinkling herself with gasoline and then igniting it. But she had not been dazed! And doesn't such a thing require an extreme amount of self-discipline? - "Unthinkable!" he exclaimed.

In any case, there were no traces of petrol in the lungs! In addition, there had been two fires, one in the rocks below the woman where the passport was burned.

Everything indicated that she had only had flammable liquid enough to burn the passport and some minor objects. On top of that, the entire background story with nine identities, and the traveling and hiding brand labels and fingerprints on all of the items. And all of the other questionable issues from the crime scene and pathology reports. Operating on that level of professionalism and still suffering from what could not even be proven to be an accident was out of the question! She had neither worn the watch nor the boots. He found it likely that somebody else had ruined the watch. Most likely it had been thrown onto the rocks and heat!

- "This is a murder! Dam it if this is not a murder!" Elated, Henriksen grabbed the phone and called Seland. After a while, the conversation was diverted to Trondheim, where he spoke to Seland on the police radio in Johannesen's car through a poor connection.

Seland did not understand all the talk about the pathology report as it came pouring out of Henriksen. He had not brought the reports and could therefore not check up on what Henriksen told him. On the plane back to Bergen, he thought through their conversation. Of course, the fact that the lungs did not contain any particles of gas could be an issue, but then they had to check the body again. He decided to talk to Dr. Garder when he returned to Bergen. However, it would not be an option to publicly go out with a murder theory now. They had no suspects and no leads on any suspects. He had no doubt that Kripos would share that opinion!

He flipped open the newest edition of the Bergen newspaper to see what they had written about his case. This headline caught his attention:
"NATO Foreign Ministers gathered in Brussels and Warsaw – The Pact in Budapest", but that was it. The Americans who had previously said they would withdraw from Europe now concluded that they would "maintain our strength in Europe for another half a year". Gromyko and Brezhnev had moved on to East Berlin with several other party leaders to meet Ulbricht and Honnecker and probably to influence them to accommodate NATO's desire for liberalization in policy of the west, he could read. Seland laid down the newspaper and let his visual attention drift away to the clouds outside.

– "Those guys live a dangerous life", he thought. - "God knows what caused the Americans to make such a decision? Judging from the reactions, the Communists did not like it whatsoever! No, I would rather have my cozy, local war with Kripos and POT!" He leaned back in the airplane seat and pulled the newspaper over his head.

Bruun could hardly do anything about the matter. The problem was, of course, that this Lenktov had been in Trondheim at the same time as the woman. "And why was that?"

He quickly decided to write off the episode as an accident, dropping out possible interrogation of the Russians and refraining from sending a complaint to the embassy, as he would then appear to be less accountable.

He contacted Seland and informed him that the information about the Russians in Trondheim was considered to have nothing to do with the case and should not be described in any reports. The decision was final and had a ministry clearance.

eland dropped the phone after Bruun had called and shook his head. – "No way we are oing to get 'all the cards on the table' in this case!" He said loudly and ironically as erger entered the door and looked at him, quite puzzled.

;ergen, December 1970

eland got two of his most talented people to review all the places where the woman had tayed to find technical traces, if possible. The two rooms 424 and 407 were at Hotel .osenkranz and Hotel Hordaheimen. But nothing of interest was found in neither of the ooms.

The investigation in Stavanger showed that a Finella Lorck had stayed at hotel vithun from November 9-18. Personal information was entered in the hotel book, but ie alien form was not found. She was assigned room 609, but after having seen it she sked to change to 615. The staff at the hotel described her as a bit "oriental". She had er hair tied together in a ponytail and was dressed in dark pants and a parka with a ood and leather lining. She often walked around in a turquoise robe well into the day. .pparently somewhat drunk.

Her passport, lt 50284, was Belgian and the series of numbers was previously ssued at the embassy in Norway. The passport turned out to be false.

The hotel staff remembered her well and the police concluded that this was the ame woman as the deceased. The descriptions were unique and largely the same. hroughout, the woman was characterized as very pretty. She spoke bad English and sped a little.

The staff from a small local shop remembered the woman well from buying a heap umbrella. In particular, the sales assistant had noticed the big green earrings. She as presented with a picture of the earrings that were found at the scene and said that iey were the same.

The umbrella found on the scene was, with a high level of certainty, traced back) the producer fa. B. Lunde in Stavanger.

Several of the hotel staff and salesmen in the stores said that the lady seemed a ttle shy. And a little sad, one of them had said.

A taxi driver had driven a lady from the hotel to the harbor. He did not doubt that iis was the same woman after reading the police description. The driver remembered ery well that the lady had been wearing new blue navy boots with laces.

He had carried her suitcase on board Vingtor and heard her mentioning "ticket". s he drove away, he saw her going into the terminal to buy a ticket. The Vingtor's assenger list showed that "Alex" had bought ticket number 57 on November 18, for ergen.

Seland had read the extensive reports from the police in Stavanger and was npressed. - "We have to do something. Those people are in need of encouragement. hey must have been working around the clock"!

Ie wrote in a remark in the report to Kripos that "the officer's efforts for 18 hours day fter day in the investigation should be acknowledged by informing the Stavanger police ffice officially about their endeavors".

Both Berger and Seland gradually began to believe that they should resolve the matter. They no longer doubted that the woman they described was the same as the one found in Isdalen valley.

- "Now it's just a matter of time before we get a breakthrough", said Berger. - "The questioning of the Germans on Neptune will provide the answer, I'm sure!"
- "Possibly", Seland answered thoughtfully. - "It depends on what you mean by answers."
- "Who she is, of course" replied Berger.
- "But what about the suicide theory and all the secrecy and why. I doubt we will ever get any answers to that. There is way too much politics, money and prestige connected to this case". Seland waved his arms outwards with a resigned movement,
- "In fact, it is always the same in these cases. When we do not get anywhere and a suicide theory is available, it's far too easy for the bosses to put the case on hold." He pointed his fingers to his chest.
- "Who the hell is the lawyer and defender for the person who committed suicide like in other murders? Who's acting on her behalf? People who are dead can say nothing, and have nobody to stand up for them in the cases where we decide that they committed suicide. Nobody seeks to verify the theory either, at least not officially."

Berger listened patiently to the frustrated outbreak and nodded repeatedly with his chin resting on the back of his hand. – "We must at least make sure the victim gets a fair chance when neither Kripos nor POT seem willing to! We are both the prosecutor and the defendant here. And it puts us in a pretty bad spot if we are wrong."

It was clear that Berger had given up on trying to follow Seland's train of thought and he continued with the briefing on the investigation. – "The Germans are sending a guy who arrives on Thursday. You and Henriksen will take that round", he said.

But it just so happened that it would not turn out that way. A short while later Kripos sent an announcement stating that the E-service would take care of all questioning of foreigners.

Rudi Listow was a Lieutenant Colonel at the German Inspection who conducted diving and catastrophe training for German submarines in the scuba dive aquariums and fire protection area at Haakonsvern. Ever since 1963 and particularly often after 1967, he had traveled regularly to Bergen to train people. On November 3, he brought a group of 30 young Germans to the Neptune hotel. The group was to attend the Haakonsvern training and was to stay at the hotel until Friday.

A local POT officer questioned Listow, who immediately remembered the woman staying at the hotel at the same time. He demonstrated her figure by hand gestures and said that he doubted that any of his countrymen had spoken to her.

Most of them went back on Friday, November 6, but four of them stayed behind. Listow offered to contact those who had returned to Germany and ask them if they knew anything.

He viewed the drawings that had been made of the woman and said that the one of her profile, wearing a feather wig came closest to her in real life. He described her as a 25-28 year old who was nicely built and had a wriggling walk. He said he recalled her wearing in a black skirt and a pullover with a round collar.

He remembered that one man sat at the same table as the woman in the dining room without noticing whether they were having a conversation or not. He seemed to remember that she chain-smoked South State. The officer looked surprised for a moment and examined Listow after the observant remark.

The four from the group who were left were also questioned. One of them remembered the woman as being "always alone", but had not noticed anything special. Nor did they know her nationality.

The other instructor thought she had a sharper nose than on the drawing and that her face was a bit fuller. Otherwise, he described her like the others. Around 25 years old, pretty figure, dark short hair, serious, smoked cigarettes, wore a folding skirt and a blouse.

The POT officer was dissatisfied with the result and decided to continue to question some of the hotel's service staff that remembered the woman, as a comparison.

An elderly waiter thought the woman was 30-40 years old. She was dressed sporty in pants and sweaters. A younger girl thought the woman was about 25 years old and said that she mostly wore skirts.

A restaurant apprentice believed she had been around 30 years old, with long dark hair and probably wearing a trouser suit. She thought the woman had spoken German.

A female cook apprentice said that the woman answered in German when she spoke English to her. She was about 25-30 years old, had her hair in a ponytail and wore a skirt with a golden chain around her waist. She thought the drawings of the dead woman looked similar but thought she had more of a curved nose.

A waiter described the woman about the same, but added that he had also seen her enter the restaurant the second time looking different, with short feathered and bright hair.

A waitress thought her face had been more narrow than the face in the drawing. She remembered having thought the woman might be an Israeli student.

A different waitress described her being around 30 years old, having long dark hair and wearing a light dress. She said she recalled her ordering halibut for one of her meals.

The POT officer remembered having read the report from Trondheim, stating among other things, that the woman had ordered halibut at a restaurant there.

Both descriptions and behavior confirmed that the woman at Neptune was the same as in Trondheim the only difference was the names.

Seland and Berger received a copy of the POT report, which was also sent to Interpol in Germany. Seland did not find any new clues in the documents. They never received an answer from Germany and Kripos later announced that they had reached their budget limit, so that questioning the Germans in Germany too was either not relevant or out of the question. The message included that since it had been confirmed that the woman was likely to have committed suicide, the police would not go through lengths to find her identity.

"That is bullshit. We have never felt completely confident with the suicide theory. And we miss the opportunity to question 30 German men who stayed here for a whole week while the woman was here. Shewas probably also German…? Something's fishy is going on! We are being blocked no matter what we do". Seland stopped for a moment.

– "I'll tell you one thing Berger", he continued, "this case can never ever be solved. For that to happen, the bar has already been set too high, and there is too much prestige involved. The case will drag on for years to no avail. At least, that is my opinion! Look here", as he slammed the report against Henriksen who entered the door. - "Read it"!

In a few hours Henriksen had skimmed through the many interviews and gained some sort of overview of and perspective on the material. What he found most deviant and strange was that no one at all had noticed anything about the characteristic scent of perfume that was a remarkable theme with this woman before. Had he not known better he would have thought that it was not the same woman! - "Hopeless"!

Another thing was that the descriptions of the face and the comparisons with the drawing were not entirely clear. Several of the testimonies were unpredictable and very different. After such a long time, and the fact that the woman was not found until one week later, made it very difficult for people to remember. Henriksen was angry, but realized that this was a reality he had to accept. He was used to this from his other cases.

Oslo, December 1970

After the Italian Tromboli, who was wanted by the sheriff in Oppdal and had had his apartment searched in Milan, suddenly appeared in Norway, apparently after a business trip in Sweden and Helsinki, the chief of Kripos, Thurmann, decided to do the questioning himself.

Tromboli was taken to the office and after a short introductory briefing, Thurmann said, - "Well, this is the case and the reason we wanted to talk to you". He stared at the Italian while supporting his left elbow with the back of his right hand on the desk and rubbed his cheeks between his thumb and middle finger.

Tromboli looked curious and seemingly surprised at him. - "Mamma Mia, police officer. If I had known this, I would never have talked to that woman. Do you really think it might be her that they found?" Thurmann did not answer but pushed a paper towards Tromboli. - "This card was found in the woman's luggage. Do you recognize it?" The card was a postcard from Norway in the winter with painted and drawn designs of sledding at Christmas time, with "Norwegian Winter" inscribed on the back.
- "I made it. There are thousands of copies of these cards throughout Scandinavia." Tromboli looked both happy and proud. – "I wrote the map in Sweden and the publisher Grafen in Oslo makes them and gets them printed at low cost in Milan. They are distributed in all of Grafen's branches in Oslo, Stockholm and Helsinki."

Thurmann studied him. The guy had to be both naive and not so narrow-minded. – "The question is, of course, whether you gave this to the dead woman yourself." He now stared at Tromboli.
- "Never! I usually have samples of my cards in the car, but I do not have this card. You can get them everywhere. That lady in Bergen may have bought it somewhere." Trumboli brushed his jacket sleeve with a nervously and looked at Thurmann resentfully.

Thurmann leaned forward again. – "As you probably know, we are familiar with the story from Kristiansand. You certainly understand that it is natural to see these

things in context. A rape accusation is not commonplace in this country." Tromboli's face slightly changed color and he straightened his neck with a quick movement.
– "I never have and will never be able to harass a woman! That was a false charge from a scorned woman and therefore the case was dropped."

The portrayal made Thurmann think of Italian-English comedy films, and that either the man was a great actor or he was really smart. – "Well, back to the picture," he continued. – "We have reason to believe that this card was not yet for sale when the woman in Bergen died." Thurmann raised his eyebrow and stared directly at Tromboli.
– "Yes, in that case I could not have had it, either!" Tromboli was clearly relieved and leaned back in the chair.

Thurmann found it unproductive to follow this subject further. "Let's go back to Oppdal, where did you travel from there?"
– "She was going to take the train to Oslo and I offered to drive her. But instead of taking the short road we traveled around the coast of Kristiansund and Åndalsnes. By the way, we ate lunch at Hotel Aleksandra in Loen. I think Berg, who is in charge, must remember us. When we came to Oslo we went to Pettersen at Grafen. He greeted the lady there. I'm sure about it. Later we joined friends in Værmdø near Stockholm. Lorett conversed a lot with one my friends, an American lady. She apparently left for Copenhagen afterwards, receiving a postcard from there after a week's time". Tromboli pushed the card further down on the desk away from himself.
– "These were taken of the deceased and are partially reconstructed", said Thurmann, pushing a pile of photos towards Tromboli.
– "I must admit that the face-images is similar. The others are quite different. And by the way, she had a lot of money in travel checks and said that she had been in Rome, Greece and the Netherlands. Where she is now I do not know. Surely somewhere in European." He looked enquiring at Thurmann but did not receive an answer.

Thurmann had terminated this part of the interrogation by leaning back in reflection without sending the Italian away. He found the whole story extremely exotic and distant from his own trivial everyday life. To randomly meet a Euro-Chinese student from South Africa on the Oppdal square and then take her on a car trip around Norway and parts of Sweden-Finland was beyond what his own Norwegian imagination could bring.

Kripos had already checked the alibi at hotels Aleksandra, Grafen and Sweden, and confirmed Tromboli's story. A telex from the South African Police in Greenstown confirmed that the closest they came to Lorett Junkin was:

"Miss Loretta Junklin is not reported missing. She is Chinese/European, and a student at Rhodes University",

Interpol in Rome had turned Tromboli's apartment upside down at the Milan address without finding any traces significant for the case. The Interpol was unaware that he also had an apartment by lake Como.

Thurmann had confirmed from Helsinki that Tromboli and his friend had been there on October 8, but he dropped a new interrogation in the case because of the unfolding of recent events. The fact that Tromboli had mentioned that Junklin had visited Rome was not very interesting now after the response from South Africa, and no new inquiry was made to Interpol.

He thought for a moment about the newspaper article about Montessori and that the representative who was sent from the Norwegian embassy in Rome had not found any connection after the visit there. Damn those ambassadors! They are not going to find anything. Our people should have gone themselves, he concluded with anger. Nevertheless, he decided to try the Italian.
- "Montessori, does it tell you anything?" he suddenly asked Tromboli.
- "Sorry, Monte what?" the Italian replied with big eyes.
- Fuck, Thurmann swore in his mind. Obviously, he was on the wrong track. Fucking crazy Italians! - "You can go", he said.

He was already feeling really tired and thinking that suicide was a good solution. He picked up the newspaper and read the latest news about the massacre of the workers at the Lenin yards in Gdansk and the other cities.

Close to 50 people had been shot by police and armed forces. Several thousand were injured and arrested. Thurmann could also read under a newspaper photo that a young electrician, Lech Walesa, waved his fist to protest the authorities' treatment of workers in the shipyard.

In the area around Bergen, the case now had almost reached cult status. Countless press releases with interviews of people who had encountered and seen the Isdal woman in the strangest places were replaced by theories of all kinds of country of origin and identities for the woman.

Seland was eventually fed up with all the phone calls and press releases. At the same time, he was annoyed and cursed Kripos and POT for no longer showing sufficient interest in the investigation. However, he still had to admit that it would be hard to believe that they could keep the attention much longer.

The case had gradually occupied three entire floors in the police department, both Crime 2's on the sixth floor and technical on the seventh and eighth floor.

The final report summary was already done. It would eventually become necessary to complete the extensive format on this investigation. They had run out of money. In front of him at the desk was the most recent list of people working overtime, with hours logged and names of all who participated in the investigation. The criminal chief had returned the list and written in uppercase letters at the bottom that "Sorry, but this does not work anymore".

Seland had already had several discussions with the management about the budget and was not surprised. Like so many times before, he was still sitting and wondering about little details concerning the case that still roamed around in the back of his mind. The small fragmented fingerprint on the broken sunglasses was in fact the only link between the woman and the suitcases at the train station. He could not help but think that this was just a thin piece of straw that easily could be torn in two.

First, there was uncertainty as to whether the impression of the burned little finger really was the same. In addition, POT was the one that had followed up on this impression. They had previously managed to borrow the pharmacy prescription from the suitcase without anyone noticing. He had a feeling of discomfort over not knowing whether they could have removed the sunglasses for a while as well. But what interest should they have in doing so? He also found the matter with the US Embassy rather puzzling.

"Maybe the case is mixed up with big politics"! he said to him self. And it was by no means impossible that all the identities and trips were related to missions of espionage. POT had in any case shown a great interest in the case! Although people in other departments were generally very interested when Crime department 2 had murder cases, so that wasn't unusual. It was hardly anything more than that in this case. Getting involved in something a little more exciting than they were used to. The young people from "traffic and order" had for example done a great job after they were assigned to help. He thought that that the people from technical on the other hand, had done a shitty job, with a few honorable exceptions.

"Solo! Solo was the name.", he exclaimed. The name on her wristwatch was a dubious association with that lady. "Well, she was most likely not as 'solo' and lonely as people believe", he muttered. An expert had identified the watch to be a boy's watch with a leather strap. Later they discovered the manufacturer, Langendorf watchmakers in Switzerland.

It was already ten o'clock in the evening, and Seland tore himself away from his thoughts and got out of the office. Early evening! He still had his wife and children waiting at home. Even though "waiting" was perhaps a strong word to use.

Further down the hallway, Henriksen was still analyzing the report from the POT. He did not doubt that the Germans in the hotel knew more than they said they did. He thought it was striking that most people almost immediately remembered the lady, but almost never connected anything special with her. One of the bosses even remembered which cigarette brand she smoked, South State!

"It shouldn't even be fucking possible to remember the cigarette brand and not the girl", he shouted loudly. "Something is completely wrong! I wouldn't be surprised if he turned out to be the guy who gave her the matches we found."

Nobody admitted having talked to her or having been in contact with her. Nevertheless, he thought the chambermaid was telling the truth when she said she heard the woman say "Ich komme bald" ("I am coming soon") to one of the Germans. The girl thought that she would recognize the German if she saw him again. But as their superiors refused to follow up with the Germans or travel down and do the questioning, there was little they could do.

Rumors were floating around that the German military E-service always had one of its people in counter-espionage in place among the navy soldiers in Bergen. First and foremost, to ensure that the STASI did not infiltrate the course service and thereby gain access to the NATO base on Haakonsvern. Henriksen shrugged his shoulders.

" It would not surprise me one bit", he thought, "it seems logical". "Kripos and POT have behaved strangely in this case. Obviously, they know something we have not been told."

He wrote his thoughts and comments down on a sheet of paper and then attached it to the report before he put it on Seland's desk on his way out of the office.

Chapter 2

ISOTOPSY
Novaja Semlja - Moscow, January 1970

Early in January, a telegraph operator on board the naval trawler, Ms. Potemkin, wa
listening in on the radio west of the Barents Sea between Hopen and Bjørnøya, when h
picked up a coded message, suspected to have come from a US submarine further eas
towards Novaja Semlja. When attempting to decode the message the operato
surprisingly received the following results:

"USS a1, port forward ballast trim. Minor default. Prod. Warnemann, Flens T".

Although the content was of little interest to him, obviously a common technica
request, he had standing orders to report everything. When the operator receive
feedback from the naval base in Haakonsvern outside Bergen in Norway on the sam
frequency two days later, the same solution was used on the code. The answer wa
handed over to the captain immediately:

"Ussmhq. Hold position and route reych isl 6.10. Control tank 20.10 7 days
Haakonsvern bgno remont 14.11 6 days. No Trans".

The two reports were immediately forwarded to the Ministry of Defense's Marin
Operations Center and forwarded to the KGB.

The relationship between the United States and the Soviet Union was very tens
at that time. The United States nuclear submarine fleet in the northern areas, with long
range nuclear missiles, was the number one headache for Russia. The USS A1 was th
command center for the fleet and had all of the information about all submarines in th
Atlantic fleet and their movements. It was also a third generation Nautilus and the U
Navy's pride.

For a long time, parts of the Soviet leadership had developed a few differen
highly prioritized strategic scenarios that could be implemented under certai
conditions.

After a brief conference between defense minister Bahria and KGB chie
Karlovich, they concluded, along with first secretary Sergey Tonkin, that the case shoul
have the highest priority. A possible disclosure of the American nuclear missile position
would be an invaluable help as a means of urgency in the Cold War and, at the very end
completely disastrous for the United States and NATO.

The deciphering of the telegram from the A1 only showed a routine low priorit
repair order routed, without any operational breaks, via Keflavik in Iceland and furthe
to the two submarines in Flensburg and Bergen.

The fact that the message confirmed the submarine to travel to two differen
workstations was the information that prompted the KGB system to immediatel
prioritize the matter.

A selection of four trusted, experienced KGB officers was promptly appointed to ake care of each of their work areas with Tonkin as the leader. The operation was given he code name Isotopsy.

The first phase was to establish contact at the shipyard in Flensburg and to gain ccess to the NATO base Haakonsvern near Bergen. Tonkin made it clear that for the ake of leaks, no one in the KGB network would in any way appear in the Norwegian reas, nor should the target of the operation be disclosed to anyone other than the lirectly involved participants.

Tonkin poured a small glass of vodka. He shrugged his shoulders and accidentally plashed some vodka on the documents from the USSR's Potemkin. He swore quietly efore he leaned back into the chair and closed his eyes.

He was 43 years old and for the first time in his career, he was to be given an ssignment that really resembled the dreams he used to have at the cadet school. He losed his eyes and leaned back in the chair before swallowing the rest of the vodka and ;rabbing the phone. He first punched in the number to Annan Lorc in Lebanon, but hanged his mind and directly called Lenktov in Odessa instead.

White frosty smoke resembled the tail of a veil on the Muscovites being driven past the Kremlin in the winter cold. On his way home, Sergeant Tonkin rubbed away the ce on the inside of the window and stared straight ahead at the road as he passed Hotel Jkraine, turned right under the Novoarbatsk Bridge and continued towards the new Southwest district. The river on the left was covered in ice and the towering university complex was barely visible through the snowstorm.

His breath clothed the windows with frost on the inside of the worn Volga that coughed" its way through on poorly ploughed streets. He felt privileged. People were villing to pay 18000 rubles for a used Volga. A new one only cost 6000, but you had to vait ten years for a new one! The thought of a life without enough money and at least a ittle bit of luxury made Tonkin nauseous! He would under no circumstances risk losing lis own privileged position and did not hesitate to act on something that could help secure his own future.

With a shrug he started to think about the summer in Odessa and Lebanon, vhere he had followed the last two years of Miss Fenella Lorcan's training from a listance. Lenktov had no doubt he had done a great job. Rarely had he seen young igents show such affection for the desire to serve their country. With her youthfulness vet adult appearance, she radiated an expression of cosmopolitan class.

He remembered the very elegancy in her movements when she jogged with the experienced KGB agent, Lenktov, along the beach with her ponytail swaying in the back.

Fenella came to know Nika, Nikolovich Lenktov, quite well from the training schools in Moscow and Odessa and from the meetings earlier this year. They eventually leveloped a relationship based on mutual admiration. Fenella fully trusted the older ind experienced thirty-seven-year-old Lenktov and he was impressed by her willingness ind efforts for the party.

The pain in Tonkin's shoulder increased and brought him back to reality with the aste of profanity in his mouth. Again, he was reminded of the night in Odessa when the order for the liquidation of the local party leader, Ivan Lorcan, and his wife was given. They had planned an escape through Turkey. At the glimpse of the shot that gave Lorcan a third eye, his wife woke up, grabbed a 30 cm long knitting pin from the bedside table ind stabbed him in his shoulder with a force so great that it made it through Tonkin's back. He still managed to fire a shot that hit her sideways against the wall, dropping her like a rag doll. Then he emptied the container with naphtha and threw a burning match on it as he closed the door. Fenella, who slept in the next room was rescued by the police and Lenktov.

An official message stated that western agents had executed the local party secretary and his wife, as they attempted to prevent them from stealing secret documents kept at the apartment. Lorcan was awarded the medal "Hero of the Soviet Union" post mortem by the Ukrainian Prime Minister, Nikita Khrushchev. The state-owned television company RTR showed an older image of Lorcan in uniform with the medal draped around his chest.

There was no doubt about Fenella's attitude towards the west after these events. Without any other close relatives, it became a relief and triumph for her to follow Lenktov's recommendation to be trained in Lebanon to become a KGB agent. She gained new identities and new names, the Lebanese Fenella Lorc.

London - Bergen, March 1970

March 1, the Russians received the very unpleasant message that US forces had invaded Cambodia. Tonkin was aware that this too would increase the pressure to succeed in the operation.

Early in March following two weeks of briefing and reviewing, with Lenktov Fenella had planned to go from Rome to London and stay there for a week.

The purpose was primarily misdirection, bringing payment to one of Tonkin's agents, while making purchases and preparations for their stay in Norway. The name of the entry pass was Nina Vinkelman and she entered the Kensington Inn under the name of Vera Zimmerman. In a brief first meeting with her English contact on a resting bench at the British Museum, she received the coded message that formally confirmed that the operation was to continue as expected and according to plan.

The USS A1 was now on its way to Iceland and the German shipyard had booked the repair for the end of October.

On Saturday morning, Tonkin had asked for Mrs. Zimmerman at the hotel, but was not able to get a hold of her.

Secret Service routinely had the Russian ambassador followed. However, they did not notice that a message was delivered to her. It was placed in a bouquet that Fenella bought from a sales wagon at the Florist's Portobello Road in Notting Hill. She brought the flowers to afternoon tea at the Waldorf Meridian hotel where she sat down with a glass of Curacao liqueur while studying the strange phenomenon of dancing couples in the restaurant so early in the day at the well-established hotel.

On Sunday morning, she went to Hyde Park and rented a deck chair in the mild spring weather. Thousands of people had found their way to the big park areas this day. As soon as she arrived from the east side she was followed by the agent that Tonkin had used to contact her upon arrival in London earlier in the week. She sat down and flipped through the newspaper in the sun. As she got a glimpse of the Englishman she recognized from earlier, she got up and left the paper with the money and the message from Tonkin on the deck chair. The man sat down quickly and put the newspaper together with his own mirror in the overcoat pocket while apparently feigning interest in watching the people enjoying the warm spring weather.

Earlier in the day, British intelligence, MI6, had gotten a simple description of the foreign woman from the hotel's service staff. On Monday morning, they sent an internal message to the embassy and to Interpol in Rome, which was the place of departure according to the notes in the hotel. Still they could not find any traces of her there, or any sense of the incident at the hotel. At the same time, Fenella was already on the plane to Geneva carrying a passport with a different name.

Two days later, MI6 received a message from the Russian embassy that the official from the meeting at the hotel had been transferred to Moscow. However, nobody anticipated that a random visit to the hotel would lead to such consequences.

In Geneva, Lenktov already had prepared Norwegian currency along with seven new passports delivered with couriers through Vienna. The most important phase of this next part of the operation was to begin in Oslo, where Fenella was to enter the Hotel Viking on March 21. She was to list as a resident of Ostende on a business trip. It was crucial for the safety of the later implementation that she got to know the biggest cities in Norway and what hotels she should use. Only Lenktov and Tonkin were informed about the journey and she would not be able to make any contact on her own initiative. Except for the local agent Lippke, who was directly instructed by Tonkin to somehow assist Fenella, Lenktov would reach out when the time was right.

Two days later, Fenella flew to Bergen with SAS and stayed at the Hotel Bristol as Claudia Tielt before switching to the Scandia Hotel near the railway station a day later, where she stayed until April 1.

The city of Bergen with its narrow alleyways and compact city center offered an international trading environment. She carefully kept lists of all of the smaller hotels, the distance to the city center, the railway station and the airport.

On the first day, she went to Trane pharmacy near the hotel to get her ointment and to visit Frederick Lippke. Lippke was Tonkin's contact and informant in western Norway, both with regards to the explosive growth in the offshore oil industry and NATO's base outside Bergen. Lippke was a useful teammate and link in an established and efficient system for dissemination of information to the Embassy in Oslo, from the rest of the country. Bergen being an old Hansa city, large parts of the population were of German and Dutch descent. Therefore no one took notice of the "un-Norwegian" name.

In cooperation with East German intelligence, the STASI, the Russians had a network of seven local agents in Norway, with direct contact to a corresponding network in Denmark, primarily through the agent working on the Danish ferries from Kristiansand. Those remaining in Norway were in Stavanger, Bergen, Trondheim, Bodø, Tromsø, and two in Oslo, one of which was in the state administration. Much of the communication went directly from the Norwegian agents via Norwegian Communist-friendly representatives abroad, primarily in West Germany.

The Russians had long been annoyed that Norway and NATO received huge sums from US intelligence services to build and operate listening stations that could reveal and control Russian nuclear bombings on Novaja Semlja. As a result, and after the NATO exercise called Polar Express two years earlier, the Russians had significantly increased their intelligence activities in Norway. The exercise led to near-encounter incidents with Soviet forces just 30 meters from the Norwegian border at the military village Boris Gleb just south of Kirkenes. The Red Army had mobilized the entire Petsjenga division and was fully prepared for all military airports on the Kola Peninsula.

Tonkin was under great pressure by his superiors to quickly sort out and increase the efficiency of the flow of information from Norway. With the help of the Italian Tromboli, who traveled to Norway all year around in association with prospect card production and its sales, Tonkin could create an effective coordination service between agents, thereby reducing risky and direct contact between these agents and the embassy in Oslo. Tromboli's route usually went through Travemynde in Germany to Trelleborg in Sweden and further along the coast of Stockholm to Trondheim and down the coast in Norway via Bergen, Stavanger and to Hirtshals in Denmark via Kristiansand. From time to time Bodø-Tromsø and parts of Finnmark were taken on a tour that included Helsinki.

Already in 1962 and because of the Cuban crisis, Tonkin was sent to Western Germany. His primary task was to ensure that secure contacts were established there and on to Denmark-Norway. Lippke was picked up from the STASI's archives because his family was still living in Berlin. In the first phase, he was pushed into completing assignments for the sake of the safety of his sister, her daughter, and the mother. Eventually, the tasks had become so many that the sheer scale of the operation itself made it impossible for Lippke to withdraw. At the same time, it was clear that the East German family was only more and more dependent on the money he sent them every month.

Fenella, who was unknown to most of these, was first served by a woman at the pharmacy, but pointed to the prescription and the little bald man in the background as if she wanted to talk to him. Lippke had been waiting for Fenella. He took her folded prescription and inside it he found a piece of paper from a note pad. The sheet contained the name of her hotel and Tonkin's name. Lippke wrote "Isdalen", the time 11:00, the date for the following day and then returned the note before picking up the cortisone ointment as prescribed on the prescription. He signed his name at the bottom.

Tonkin had asked Lippke to meet Fenella in the area just outside the city center to establish contact and decide how to cooperate further. At the same time, one of Fenella's main tasks was to find and mark a meeting point for the end of the operation in November. Wise from experience, Tonkin had asked Lippke to find a place far away from the highway, while simultaneously having an alternative escape route.

The next morning, Fenella took the bus from the railway station up to the entrance to Isdalen. A path led inward from the last houses at the entrance of Isdalen valley and led out of the noise and away from the city. After having walked a short while, she caught sight of Lippke, who was elegantly dressed in a trekking outfit made from tweed and wearing a matching cap. She followed him from a distance. After a twenty-minute brisk walk he turned right off the road that went uphill before moving further on a narrow road over a bridge and into the forest. After about ten more minutes, he turned on to a trail that led up to the valley. Fenella caught up with him away from the main path and in between the trees. They sat down on some stones to rest and have a conversation. The place was ideal as a waiting and meeting spot, easily accessible and yet fully shielded. In addition, it was possible to backtrack on the road a little and then go north of the mountain and thus back in to town, if necessary.

The beautiful nature and the warming sun drew Fenella's mind away from reality for a moment, causing her to smile about life's melancholy. Lippke told her that the road to the valley had been built by the German military during the occupation in World War II. They had built it to ease access to large storages of ammunition. The narrow valley made an attack from the air almost impossible. He also told her that around a century ago, a composer and violinist named Ole Bull had frequently visited this place to compose music and play his violin. - "He is thought to have composed his musical piece In lonely times (I ensomme stunder) right over there", he said as he showed Fenella where the composition had taken plac.

They continued talking and agreed to set the meetings some time in November, preferably daily, right after the pharmacy closed at 17:00. Fenella was to come to the pharmacy and buy something in order for Lippke to know that she had returned. He would continue to keep Tonkin informed about fleet movements and arrivals to Haakonsvern as it lay close to his home.

Fenella drew a simple sketch of a map over the terrain they had gone through and across the paths. She handed Lippke an envelope from Tonkin with 3000 krones in Norwegian banknotes, before they individually returned downhill.

At 08:00 the next morning, she left Bergen on a boat called Vingtor along the coast and south to Stavanger. She could not help but to throw a long glance into the fjord as the boat passed the naval base Haakonsvern. The express bus with Fenella as a passenger left Stavanger at 13:30 via Kristiansand-Hirtshals-Flensburg-Hamburg with a final stop in Basel, Switzerland.

For safety reasons, Fenella had become acquainted with the name, description and password of the agent from Kristiansand on the Danish ferry, but Tonkin had explicitly asked her to avoid contacting him except in a potential emergency. Because of the disclosure of the Norwegian spy, Selmer Nielsen two years earlier, Tonkin was extremely cautious. Mere coincidence had caused the Norwegian Monitoring Center in Oslo, to miss the connection with Tonkin's other contact network in Norway. The two agents in Oslo also communicated via the Embassy's own circles and therefore had no direct contact with Tromboli.

On arrival to Flensburg at 11:00 the next day, Fenella left the bus and took a taxi directly to the little pub Beathe Uhse, where she immediately found a suitable table at the far right where she could monitor the front door. After orientating herself and drinking a quick cup of coffee, she returned to the waiting taxi and asked to be put off at the railway station. One day later she was back in Rome.

Chapter 3

C.I.A - P.O.T
Flensburg, April 1970

At the end of April, Fenella Lorc left Rome and arrived to Flensburg on April 23, to meet an important local contact as planned. She had never met Gerber and knew little about his background, except that he had no ideological standpoint as a basis for participating in operations like this one. She despised people who sold themselves for money. She had no confidence in them when push came to shove.

Ten to fifteen people were already sitting around the bar and at some of the tables. The porn business of Beate Uhse attracted marines and commuters from large parts of the region around the free port and the city port of Flensburg, not least from the areas around the base and shipyards. Uhse, who had escaped to Denmark after being a fighter in Hitler's Luftwaffe, had since the war built up in Flensburg to become Germany's uncrowned porn queen, with a significant amount of business across Europe.

For Tonkin, the place was naturally a discovery and very suitable for acquiring contacts and information about the north German marine's whereabouts. Young submarine crews were trained in these areas. The instructors were regular guests in their spare time, and the students learned to behave much like their teachers.

Tonkin had already gotten contacts on a level that made it possible for him to get involved in several of NATO's naval bases around Europe. For example, the German new submarine crews were regularly sent to Norway to train in one of NATO's best facilities, Haakonsvern base in Bergen, where they were trained in diving in shallow waters.

Early in the evening, it was still relatively quiet in the inn part of the local business. Fenella ordered half a chicken salad and a cup of coffee and sat down at the table near the door she had familiarized herself with on the short visit in March. Wearing a dark smooth wig and heavy makeup, she was hardly going to be much different from those who would gather there later in the evening. Over the bar were loads of emblems and pennants from marine vessels and cities from all over the world.
- "Typically macho", she hissed to herself with narrow lips. She discreetly picked her teeth with the matches from the box on the table before she put it in the bag.

Gerber looked as unexciting as his name implied and his photo has indicated. He immediately saw Fenella sitting alone, and after having gotten a beer at the bar he approached her table with a nervous smile on his face. - "Is this seat free, fraulein" Fenella nodded and Gerber sat down.
- "This seems to be your first time here. Are you on a journey?", he asked attentively.
– "I'm on my way to Rome and just wanted to visit the school of Montessori before moving on", she replied. The contact was established, and it sickened Fenella how clearly Gerber showed his relieve. He looked at her as he stretched out his hand that smelled of oil, sweat and beer. - "Gerber here", he said with a satisfied and insecure grin.
- "Maybe we should go to the car?" Fenella nodded as they stood up and left.

Gerber's mission in the operation was to make sure that Watson, who was Tonkin's left hand, was called to calibrate and verify the submarine repairs. Fenella had brought 20,000 German marks that she handed him when they had sat in his car. The emaining 20,000 he would receive if everything went as planned in Bergen. Tonkin had or a long time used Gerber in various contexts and paid each time, so that Gerber had ot yet become aware of his exposed position. Together with the money he followed a imple instruction from Tonkin. Fenella asked Gerber to memorize and destroy the message. Gerber nodded greedily. He dropped her near the train station where she took he train to Munich and flew to Rome.

Rome, May 1970

Rome, the old world's natural headquarters and its new undisputed treasury with the apacy as a shining gem under its wings was spectacular. But even so, Fenella was mmensely bored during her stay.

High up on the roof terrace of Palazzo Centauria, with a view of St. Peter's owering dome and thousands of red-yellow Roman rooftops, the descending evening, he felt as if the sun was her only friend. The air was filled with her own Estee Lauder mixed with the fragrance from the blossoming Gardenia that grew nearby. A glass of red ine stood on top of the table and the liquid seemed to glow in the flickering rays of unset. She lay back in the deck chair with her eyes closed while her mind slipped back o the beautiful summers in Odessa. But only a short moment later she sat up again. taly was at least equally good. - "Better!", she said to herself.

With the Communist Party with more than thirty percent support, the country was in a pecial position. Oddly enough, after the invasion of Czechoslovakia two years earlier nd the riots associated with students and workers in '68 and '69, the party had trengthened. But communism here in Italy was different from the one she believed in. t home in Moscow and Leningrad, a new wave of Stalinism flourished with Tolstikov as he leader. After a loosening up in the Khrushchev period, the system where people nformed on each other was on its way back. The invasion of Czechoslovakia was largely nknown to most Russians. Probably it was because living conditions generally dulled eople's appetite for politics. Only a few Russians took the trouble to understand the ignificance of the invasion in Czechoslovakia.

Italian communists were liberal, not least in relation to Soviet activities, more ractical and masters in adapting to a capitalist lifestyle. The party willingly cooperated ith the democrats and fully committed to Italy's NATO membership. Fenella did not ke this. Through the local newspapers she had seen that the Radical Party had an xtraordinary congress in Rome right now and that they would bow to democracy and ot encourage blank voting at the election.

"Puh! Radical!" Fenella fretted.

In the back of her mind there was hatred against compliance and disloyalty gainst the ideologies. She would never fall for the temptation to renounce her attitude owards capitalism's worthlessness. After her father's death, she had sworn never again o get attached to people or things. "You can only lose what you love" had been written n the ribbon she lay over her father's chest.

Lenktov had provided her with enough money for a long life without any worries, f she had only been able to. However, the time to stay in Chur would be difficult to fill. Being inactive was a new and troublesome dimension that she had little or no training in. To spend money and be "free" in a capitalist world did not make the situation any better.

She could not hang around too much with Watson. The risk that their meetings at the school of Montessori could be noticed was too high for them to have daily contact. After talking to Lenktov, she had decided, to travel around, both for the change in scenery and for being mobile for safety reasons. She would meet Watson in mid-June.

The sun had set and she noticed that she was freezing. She felt somewhat better at the idea of meeting Watson again and decided to make the best of the situation.

The next day she went out to the seaside resort of Forte dei Marmi in Tuscany. The city was a typical place for youth where hundreds of youngsters gathered around the piazza until late night. However, for Fenella, with her rigorous upbringing and a very serious assignment to complete, a playful and carefree attitude like this quickly became meaningless. Still she had to admit it was a little relaxing and even entertaining.

Milan, May 1970

Between May 25 and 27, Milan and Rome received visits by German-Russian Svjatoslav Richter who performed music by Beethoven and Schumann. Fenella attended his concert at the Olimpico Theater in Milan. She had the feeling that quite a few of the audience were Russians, but got a glimpse of the French defense minister that she recognized after having seen him on television. He was sitting with a group of businessmen, or probably politicians, who were to attend the next day's NATO ministerial meeting in Milan.

- "Ironically", Fenella thought. "Here I am a few meters from several of them. In a few months, they would break into a cold sweat at the very thought, if they knew about it. And the theme of the conference is force disarmament in Europe. Would they be just as keen, after the implementation of Operation Isotopsy?"

She sat down in the chair and enjoyed Richter's piano interpretation of Beethoven's piano concert in D major. In the following weeks, Fenella was to travel as a tourist on holidays between the beautiful cities of Vienna, Venice, and Nice. She had no contact with the organization and felt very alone. The agreement with Tonkin and Lenktov was reached. If they needed to contact her, they would let her know. Most importantly, she was not stationary, but in motion and had different identities.

She could sit for hours and gaze at the sea view from the window on the fourth floor of the Park Hotel in the center of Nice. French people in Provence undoubtedly have an opportunity for a good life she thought to herself and pictured Sunday afternoons with retirees playing cards and boules players between the big trees in the countryside.

But the revolt in the Latin Quarter in Paris two years ago, where more than 400 students were wounded in battle with the police and de Gaulle's 5th Republic lost, showed that the revolutionary spirit was still alive in the French people.

"Perhaps more alive than in Russia", she nodded and let her mind set sail into the azure blue sea and sky of the Mediterranean.

Following Tonkin's suggestion, Fenella succeeded to catch the Rolling Stones concert at Palazzo Dello Sport in Milan and she took another couple of trips to Nice and Venice.

Zurich - September 1970

On a Sunday morning in mid-September 1970, the little Swiss village of Chur was draped in silence, despite the chimes of the beautiful little churches that lay close to the houses in the Alpine valley.

The white curtains slowly moved in the open windows of room 312 at Internationale Hotelschüle where Fenella Lorc packed her last things before taking a taxi to the railway station to catch the train that left Chur at 12:15 for Zurich. The view over beautiful Zurich Zee was almost unreal and took her mind off what was ahead of her.

A total of 36 nations were represented at the school, from the East, the United States, Scandinavia, and Europe. Fenella was officially enrolled at the school as a Lebanese citizen after living briefly with one of the KGB agents, under the cover of him being her uncle. At home in Lebanon, Annan Lorc was apparently proud to be able to tell his friends and business associates about his "niece" that he had sent to study in Switzerland. In reality, he was completely ignorant of who Fenella was or where she came from, but it did not matter.

Kelly Young was a student who had traveled back the day before, from Zurich via Bergen in Norway to New York. They had met each other for the first time two years earlier, at the school camp just outside Beirut. Kelly was in Lebanon as an exchange student. This 24 year old was pretty straightforward and there were few traces left of her Russian upbringing in Odessa, Ukraine, as she had been adopted into an American family.

At exactly 13:20 the Swiss SSB train left for Lugano and at five o'clock that afternoon her luggage was in place in the hotel room overlooking the lakefront and the Swiss part of Lake Locarno. She knew that Lenktov would come and pick her up at 18:00 as agreed. The air-conditioning on the train journey caused an old nuisance to return. It dried out the skin along the nose and parts of her face. She now had enough time to go out and buy skin ointment at the pharmacy before Lenktov arrived.

Nika Lenktov phoned from the front desk and waited for her in the car, a Simca with Italian license plates. He greeted her warmly and hugged her with a heartfelt hug. They eagerly talked about everything that had happened since the last time they were together and behaved like the two half-in-love friends they might in fact be.

Como was just half an hour's drive away across the border. The meeting with the Italian Tromboli was very important. To ensure that the journey could not be tracked, a bundle of professionally made passports and papers had to be provided.

Fenella was informed that Tromboli regularly traveled around Scandinavia as an Italian natural illustrator and produced and sold photo-postcards with his Norwegian landscape motives. That he also had delivered the KGB's most comprehensive photo registration of Norwegian defense units was another matter. Like most Italians, he was very fond of women and had already been reported to the police once. For this reason, and for the sake of retaining general anonymity in the mission, it was very important to prohibit the Italian police from seeing the connection between the two visitors, herself, Lenktin, and Tromboli.

Lenktov parked inches from the house wall in an alley at the harbor and both quickly entered a door that was half open, before going up two floors in an old brick house. After three attempts at the doorbell, Giovanni Tromboli opened the door and exclaimed: - "Ciao, bella Fenella – and Nika". Tromboli was overflowing as usual. Fenella had met Tromboli twice before and found him quite nice.

In the elegant living room a woman in her late twenties and a man in his forties sat waiting. Both greeted them and presented themselves to Fenella. The woman introduced herself as Zana Jankaan and said she was Tromboli's secretary and traveling partner.

The man, with a somewhat feigned heartfelt smile, said he was Chargé d' Affaires Sergei Tonkin at the Russian Embassy in Milan. Fenella sensed that his smile did not reach his eyes and started to feel a little tense.

Zana's smile seemed authentic and friendly on the other hand. She handed Fenella a drink, then bent forward and gave her a warm hug with her right cheek towards her. Lenktov obviously knew Zana and Tromboli from before and everyone immediately went into the dining room where the table was covered with different maps and some airplane tickets.

Fenella had never met Tonkin face to face, even though they had contacted each other both by telephone and through Lenktov. Tonkin carefully observed her and was clearly pleased with the meeting. Tromboli randomly put his arm around her shoulder as they stood bent over the table and went through the plans. Apart from Tromboli's somewhat forced Italian gestures and acclaimed talking, the four of them were highly professional and effective.

Tonkin initiated the briefing. - "None, other than the five of us and Watson has so far been informed about this operation, neither in Italy nor Norway. Only a small group in the Supreme Soviet, including the chairman, is familiar with the plans."

With a sharp look at Tromboli, which clearly irritated him with his slightly sloppy way of communicating, he continued. - "Any mishap will be fatal to all involved. It should be clear to you that this assignment is prioritized at the highest level and above all other intelligence operations in any country in the world over the coming months". His left shoulder twitched a little as he continued. – "We are simply hostages in a power-policy game – and we have to gain the overhand. The devil is on the loose in the Middle East and Africa, and only our good relationship with Nasser prevents Americans from doing whatever they want".

He looked disapprovingly at Zana, who was about to finish the rest of her drink. - "If something goes wrong along the way, there is no easy way back for any of us. Any trace of our activities that can lead to Moscow, both during and after the operation, will be equally devastating."

Fenella studied Tonkin. Apparently without any feelings, but behind the facade, was a watchful eye. She was fascinated by the well behaved and alert man and what he stood for and could not help following his eyes when he spoke. Everything she had trained for, everything she was compassionate about, everything had been stored and was now ready to be put into action. Any disturbing element against the plans would be terminated. Nothing would prevent her from completing her task to the last detail. Tonkin, who felt Fenella's concentrated attention, continued.

– "We will hardly meet again before November in Norway. Tromboli and Zana travel in September. All further contact will be through direct meetings following the plan, also with our American and Swiss friends. We will be regularly informed by our Norwegian

ents, but only in case of emergency will they be in contact with Fenella Lore and vice versa". He nodded weakly towards Fenella.

"First and foremost, the contact for both parties will be through Tromboli. We have no reason to believe that the CIA will prepare the A1 submarine's arrival to Flensburg, considering the risk of possible intelligence operations from our side. Through our contacts at the embassy, we are aware that the Americans plan to present the visit as a disarmament mission for maintenance purposes. That is, they will officially assert that there are no nuclear weapons on board. Any intelligence activity on their part will put this into doubt. Which means we can probably work peacefully with our planned activities! I myself travel back to Milan tonight. Fenella checks in to Bellevue Resorta before taking the train to Milan and onwards to Rome tomorrow. Questions?" Again, his left shoulder moved slightly.

With eight months of careful planning and a thorough review of the plans, it was unnecessary to ask. Like the rest of them, Lenktov had an almost photographic internal overview of the entire operation.

"Okay, Tovaritsj Tonkin. We all have what we need and know what is required. I travel back to Lugano later this evening with Zana on Fenella's passport, and she brings herself unseen back over to Locarno tomorrow. Thus, Fenella's departure cannot be traced. Good luck everybody!"

Tonkin went with Fenella in the car and followed her into the hotel. As he got into the car again, he became aware that he had been observed. Just to be safe, he drove the car around the hotel and went back to check before driving back to the apartment in Milan. Back in the apartment, after Lenktov and Zana had left, Tromboli still felt Tonkin's intense look. He moved his fingers thoughtfully through his mustache, shook his head and decided to stop pursuing it.

"Not on this level", he said loudly to himself. Tonkin could not possibly suspect any of the participants?" Later that evening he was reassured by Tonkin who called and informed him that he and Fenella had been observed at the hotel. He asked him to fix the matter. Tromboli was radiating with confidence for their trust in him.

A week later, Lenktov cleared the office in Milan and brought what he needed in a smaller briefcase. The first phase was over. Tromboli and Zana had already traveled to Scandinavia.

The day before, Tonkin had flown to Bonn and drove from the news agency Tass' office to Berlin and to an apparently long-lasting summer stay at the Baltic Sea just south of Flensburg.

Lenktov pondered the international troubled conditions of late and what it would mean for their own freedom of action. Former Foreign Minister, Willy Brandt, had now been made German Chancellor and that would probably cause any leaks to the Americans about the operation to be monitored if the KGB's long-standing contact in the social circles around Brandt could be maintained.

The announcement of Nassers' death and the shipment of 5000 new Soviet observers to Egypt added further pressure on the East-West relationship and reinforced the need for them to succeed in their operation in Norway.

He looked forward to meeting Fenella again in Geneva and at a glimpse remembered their first meeting with American writer John Watson who was picking up the children of the chief of the pressure test laboratory in the Montessori kindergarten, Casa dei Bambini, in Rome. A weak feeling of discomfort flowed over him regarding the

self-assured American. He did not like the fact that even in the kindergarten h
obviously had been armed with a gun in an armpit holster under the coat. Moscow, an
not least Tonkin, had given the highest degree of trust and confidence in the operatior
With American Kelly Young as a link between them, Watson and Fenella became mor
concerned with each other than Lenktov appreciated. However, he shrugged hi
shoulders and laughed away the unfamiliar feeling.

Rome, September 1970

At the US Embassy in Rome at the end of September it was routinely registered that th
KGB officer Tonkin was back and had a higher activity level than usual. Howevei
because he left Rome and traveled to Berlin, only a brief note of this was sent to th
Central Intelligence Agency – CIA in the United States. Two days later a report appeare
from Milan saying that a local agent was believed to have recognized Tonkin in a ca
with a woman at Bellevue in Como near the Swiss border. The report was forwarded t
the CIA headquarters in Langley and was filed together with a previous request to Rom
from MI6 about the London woman.

    A few days later, the file appeared as one of several ongoing cases witl
Commander Jeff Conahan in the European OREA, the CIA Office of Russian ano
European Analysis. He read it and wondered if there could be any connection, whil
recalling Tonkin as a cynic and a "cold fish" who was not the kind of guy to mov
randomly in the outskirts of Italy. He looked him up in the personal archive ano
confirmed the suspicion that Tonkin was "probably homosexual".

    It was unlikely that he was romantically involved with a woman. - "Something"
going on", he said to himself before calling Berlin. However, no one had registere
where Tonkin was located, except for the airlines own registration.

    Conahan continued to call around and asked his embassy contact in Rome to pu
pressure on the only reliable external intelligence informant he had in Italy, Zan
Jankaan.

    Zana was raised in South Africa, but without approved citizenship and long-term
residence in Italy, France, or Switzerland, she was stateless and non-existent as a citizei
in any of these countries. She had assisted the US Embassy several times with lesse
local intelligence missions. Conahan did not know with certainty, but thought her to b
about thirty years old. However, no one had met her and all communication wen
through a sophisticated patchwork system that was retrieved from the old school c
Montessori. Thus far, Conahan considered her to be reliable. They were also aware tha
she had assignments for other non-western embassies but chose to play the game ano
considered it a source of additional information for them selves.

- "Hm. Mysterious women" he muttered. - "But could it indeed have been her, both ii
London and in Como?"

    He put voice to his thoughts again with the description from London in mind
The answer that came the next morning was negative. Zana was not to be tracked dow
at any address nor could they confirm or dismiss whether she had stayed in Italy. Th
same was true for Tonkin. Conahan sat down to write and let his mind run.

"There is something fishy going on! Jankaan and Tonkin disappeared sporadically and he casual woman in London and a homosexual Russian at a get-together specifically for women in northern Italy is too much to be considered normal."

Tonkin was a master in obtaining informants. Conahan remembered the time when Tonkin was appointed as a journalist at the Russian telegram agency Tass in Bonn, where neither the CIA nor German intelligence managed to find evidence that he worked as a professional spy. This, even though they were convinced that Tonkin had built up a network of agents throughout West Germany with branches in Denmark and Norway. In addition to acquiring contacts with radical youth at the Rostock festival and business people at the Leipzig fair, the method was, in cooperation with East German Stasi, primarily to find people who were separated from their East German family after the war or, according to the archives, secretly had benefited by cooperating with the Nazis. They were then recklessly pressured to work for Tonkin who was smart enough to make sure they were paid for the assignments. The network became self-sufficient, based on fear and eventually addiction.

Conahan was a tough leader with long experience in military and civil intelligence. After many years in the US Navy in operational leadership worldwide, he was appointed as assistant for national security affairs under vice president Nixon in 1957, while only 35 years old. Later, after serving a period as assistant chief of staff for the US Marine Corps and a brief period as operational commander in the Navy's amphibian troops in Vietnam, III Force, he had worked continuously in OREA in charge of European-Russian intelligence cases. No major political, economic, social or military change in the area avoided OREAS's attention.

Once the wanted notice had been completed, he sent it to Interpol in Paris, London, Rome, and Berlin and to the FBI in New York. At the same time, he made sure he called for an ad hoc meeting in the department and brought the case to the top of the priority list.

In Como, Italy that same afternoon, the police picked up a grossly mistreated male corpse from the sea. Identity could not be determined. Parts of the face and both hands were torn away, probably because of a mishap with a boat propeller. No local people were reported missing.

New York, September 1970

The journey from Bergen to New York with an SAS DC9 took about 10 hours and provided Kelly Young with ample time to think, before landing at Kennedy Airport. In the transit hall at Flesland airport in Bergen she had received a coded message to Brit Jonsdottir in Iceland.

The message was written on a wrapped white napkin and would hopefully be handed over to her adopted brother, technical sub-officer Phil Young aboard the USS A1 nuclear submarine. She would call Brit from a public telephone immediately after she returned to the United States and she hope to hear from Phil soon to be able to deliver the message to him. Kelly did not know the content of the message, but Fenella and Lenktov had briefed her about the repair in Flensburg and how crucial it was that the contact on board was established.

With all the technical innovations in defense, she realized that it was important for the Russians to keep her informed, and at the same time she had the same conviction as all other spy agents had "the more they know about each other, the safer it is". Even though she had a foot in each continent – America and Europe - she had a strong feeling for her country of birth. She felt she was making a contribution to helping both parties.

Phil's parents – and her adopted parents, had died in a car accident three years ago. Kelly had a good relationship with her adopted brother Phil, especially after their parents died. After he joined the US Navy, they only saw each other between his missions.

Kelly and Phil shared their parents' large apartment in Greenwich Village. She took the airport bus to the city and a taxi home to the apartment. Shortly after arriving home, she called Papadakis at the Spartakus restaurant on 23rd Street and told him that she was back from school in Switzerland. Kelly spoke almost fluent Greek and assumed that was why she had gotten the job at Spartakus.

During their stay in Beirut, Fenella, instrumented by Tonkin, had told her about this renowned restaurant. What she didn't know was that she had been recommended to Papadakis via the contact network through the Embassy in Athens.

Being raised by Ukrainian immigrant parents, Phil shared Kelly's political views. Both had been strongly provoked by the communist flames in the United States in the 60's but hadn't been a part of any protest group. As a young college student, Kelly became involved in the radical society at Columbia University. In 1969 a wave of bomb threats and attacks took place across the United States. In Seattle alone a total of 54 bombs exploded. In New York, police and fire stations were terrorist targets, and two houses were blown up in Greenwich Village, near Kelly and Phil's apartment. "The bomb man" Ted Gold was killed in the explosion and Kathy Wilkinson escaped abroad.

Kelly was quite shocked after the events and didn't reconnect with Fenella for a while. Phil left on a mission and Kelly travelled to Europe, first on vacation and then to the Hotel and Restaurant School in Switzerland, sponsored by Papadakis.

She received an overwhelming reception when she returned to work at Papadakis. Jovial Papadakis himself, embraced her dearly before dragging her along as he marched around in the premises and praised her in front of all the guests. - "This is our new restaurant expert directly from Switzerland's best hotel school!", he said proudly.

Kelly started re-integrating and soon enough she was back in her New York routine. During lunch breaks for a few days the following week, she left the restaurant and called Brit from a payphone nearby. They exchanged the latest news about the holiday and school and Brit thanked her for the letter, both perfectly aware that they were speaking code.

- "I am sure you have plenty of marines from the base to flirt with, to help you through the cold winter. And if Phil were to pop up, I know him well enough to tell you that he will end up in the Blue lagoon after such a long time under cover."

Kelly assumed that Brit had received the message and stopped talking about Switzerland and school before they expressed mutual wishes to meet again as soon as possible.

Early on the morning on October 6, the USS A1 submarine docked at the American Keflavik Base at Reykjavik, Iceland. The next day, landing permits were granted to most of the crew, after months at sea. Half of the crew was replaced by a new one already waiting in Iceland.

Phil called Kelly from the base as soon as he landed. They talked about this and that and she told him how happy she was to be back home. She then told him that after all the hard work he deserved to swim around in the warm water at the Blue Lagoon and check out the girls.

- "In case you meet my friend Brit from Switzerland, please give her my best." Phil understood the hint and immediately realized that he should contact her. - "Sure!" he replied before wishing her well and promising to call again before boarding again.

In the afternoon Brit registered that the guest had received a landing permit. She knew what the next step was, so she went to the Blue lagoon. Brit had seen pictures of Phil during her and Kelly's stay in Switzerland so she immediately recognized him when he arrived to the lagoon.

- "Hi, I'm Brit", Phil heard a low voice. A blond Icelandic woman in a bikini stood up smiling in the shallow water in front of Phil. He had never seen her before and could not help but be surprised.

When Phil had gone to the command school, Brit had borrowed his room, but they had never had the opportunity to meet before. They got out of the water together and dried off in the cold misty air.

Later they sat down at a table in the little cafe. She bought two hamburgers and asked Phil to take good care of the extra napkin. They sat and enjoyed their time together, sharing stories from America and her time there, until it was time for him to go back to the base.

The coded message on the napkin that he got form Brit, with instructions from Lenktov, gave Phil the necessary information about the repair at the Warneman workshop in Flensburg, the base in Bergen, and that Watson and Geber would be the contacts. His own task in the operation would be to get the micro photo. The device would be smuggled aboard in Bergen. With Kelly involved and Lenktov in the scene, he felt no aversion to the task. Phil smiled at the thought of meeting the beautiful girl from the Blue lagoon once again.

Chapter 4

USS A1
Flensburg, October 1970

The soundless and yet majestic, 186-meter-long submarine A1 seemed like a blend of a giant shark and a whale as it moved through the narrow waters around Skagen, 150 feet below the surface, on its way to Øresund in Denmark. The speed was logged at 22 knots, but the submarine did not give off any more noise than the snoring from the crew that could clearly be heard in the kitchen where the preparations were underway for an early breakfast.

Only one third of the crew was on duty. After submerging underwater at Grenen, the submarine took a southwards course, parallel about two degrees east of the civilian shipping company. A few hours later it crossed Grenå on its way into Storebelt with a course past Odense. The speed was set to 14 knots while the depth was reduced to 110 feet.

Quartermaster Phil Young had spent the last few hours standing in the sonar room of the attack center. The landslide in the shallow waters around Denmark did not allow much time for thinking about anything besides following the sonar. Much like his fellow submariners, Phil was fully aware of his role and importance on board and that the entire ship was dependent on his effort as an individual. In combat situations, as in peace missions, the people were responsible for themselves and for each other. It was the crew that made the A1 a ship.

He had been trained in managing himself and trusting that his shipmates performed their duties in the same way, developed the operational creatures of almost 120 heads who always had control over the ship.

Upon passing Odense, Phil heard the commander, Commander A.F. Janson, as he went through the control room on his way up to the attack center to take over the command at the long entrance to Flensburg. He sat down and threw the key and the folder on the counter at the periscope eye, "the Conn". Immediately, the depth was up to about 25 feet. Phil's own guard was simultaneously taken over by Lieutenant Corbin. Corbin went straight to the navigation center, just behind the periscope slot.

At a glimpse, the idea of the repairs came to Phil's mind as he pushed the short piece into the control room and passed the ballast control. In a soap bar, among the other belongings at his bunk, there was already a perfect impression of the key to Janson's cabins. He heard about the port authorities' entry orders from the radio room on the starboard side before he went to the galley to pick up a cup of coffee.

In the international waters of Skagerak north of Swedish Skåne and Danish Sjælland, the USSR Vostok had been in a waiting position for almost three days. As soon as the A1 passed the radio message, Captain Voltov received the message from Moscow and went to seven meters periscope to take in air and recharge the generators. Shortly after that, Vostok went down to 90 feet and headed south with a speed of 16 knots. Voltov was ordered to await the situation in the Baltic Sea at a position between Bornholm and Rugen in Germany. In the weeks before, Voltov had been preparing in the waters off Gdansk in Poland. The Russians had big problems with riots, and there were attempts to organize a strike committee on the big Lenin yard in Gdansk. Voltov id not know the cause of the turmoil but had been informed that the riots had spread to dynia and Szczecin.

Because of the A1's call to Flensburg, which the Americans could hardly hide after rrival, a new order from Moscow was given that the A1 operation should have priority at all costs" and that "attack order" to stop the riots on the Lenin yard should be ostponed to the beginning of December.

The Vostok was of the Foxtrot class, built two years earlier at the Novo-dmiralteysky yard in Leningrad. The ship was powered by oil with 75 men and 32 orpedoes aboard, six of which ready in the launchers.

The submarine was able to last fully immersed for three days, which made life on oard quite restricted. The working days and nights were characterized by six hour hifts for everyone on board, including the officers. They were not able to exercise on oard, as the ship had only three toilets and shower facilities with seawater for the crew vere available only every three days.

Captain Voltov was proud to lead one of Soviet's most advanced tactical ubmarines. Life on board was like a different world and in his opinion the esponsibility that rested on the submarine captain was considerably larger than that which rested on a naval captain. He felt honored and undoubtedly privileged to have een entrusted with this responsibility. As an old navigational officer he found himself the map and navigation room in front of the control room. Voltov knew the Baltic Sea nd the areas along the coast Germany, Sweden, and Denmark better than their own abins.

The Danes kept close control of all submarines traffic. A Danish military ntelligence officer had already sent notice to the A1 that a submarine of the Foxtrot lass had left the island of Øresund three days earlier.

Because of the situation in Poland, the United States intelligence service and JATO made its best ensure that the USS A1 was not on any casual visit to Poland in the outheastern Baltic region. It was assumed that the Russians would look at the presence the context of the developments in Gdansk. The A1 therefore went early on a surface osition on arrival to Flensburg and received official German political visitors by the ock along the shipyard shortly after arrival.

Although the Russians realized that this was a game and that A1 needed repair, it id not make the political impact any less and they were not happy to read about the isit in the newspapers. The East German STASI, who carefully followed the events vithout having the same information as the Russians, where far from happy and arlovich expressed his anger in his daily message to Tonkin.

Gerber had done his job and made sure that John Watson had arrived at the hipyard as a specialist a week earlier to participate in the repair on the A1. Following erber's recommendation for technical assistance in the review and calibration of the allast automation, personnel clearance was provided for Watson to work in the navy ubmarines. Primarily, it was the sensitive trimming tanks that required special xpertise. As Watson had previously been hired to do this kind of work, he blended into he environment quite smoothly.

Commander Janson took the red operating folder under his arm and went down o his private cabin to change uniform as soon as the ship had surfaced. His cabin was he only room on board where he could lock the door. He kept the operating protocols nder the bedspread in the locked cabin when he was out of the ship. Phil Young and the other sub-officers had noticed and used make jokes about Janson sleeping with the entire Atlantic fleet between his legs.

Gerber and Watson together with two people from the shipyard management were among the first to come on board. Watson knew Young from photos Tonkin had shown him and looked closely at members of the submarine crew as he passed them. Phil sat in the hallway and browsed through newspapers that had just been brought. He kept close watch on everyone who boarded. They caught sight of each other at the same time and Watson smiled and greeted and presented himself while sounding like an American. He asked if he could have a cup of coffee while they waited for the machine chief and his assistants to get an indication of the damage.

The heavy bag, full of measuring equipment and tools, was put on the floor just next to Phil. The four dockyard people talked to the crew in the hall about the latest news and where to go when they got the landing permit. Using a newspaper as a cover, Phil let the soap bar slide unnoticed into the half-opened bag.

Gerber and Watson sat in the officer's district for several hours and reviewed the data and observations the engineers had done before taking a quick technical look in the control room to investigate the problem. They left the ship late in the afternoon after discussed the progress and schedule for the repair with Janson and Corbin.

Late that evening, Watson received the key casting along with a glass of beer at the cafe "Uhse". He sat at the table Fenella had chosen and studied the room until he saw Phil Young glancing at him before entering the toilet. Watson followed and the newly acquired key changed hands.

Back at the table he murmured to himself, -"Germans are effective beyond doubt but so are Americans." He felt that the first critical phase was over. It would be very necessary to secure the key first, in case it did not fit and they had to try again.

When Phil arrived later in the evening with the key in his own possession, most of the officers and Janson were still at the cocktail party at the German Baltic fleet admiral's party. Unnoticed, Phil put the key into the lock on the door of the captain's cabin and made sure it fit. He continued to his own place and knew that the events had taken place. The uniform coat was dark with sweat under the armpits. He slept like a stone when Janson and the others came in.

Paris - Norway, October 1970

The waiting period after the meeting in Como was finally over for Fenella. At the end of October, she travelled to the Regina hotel in Geneva and the following day to Paris in Calais and Altona where she met Lenktov.

The evening in Paris was the last before the crucial operation in Norway. Both of them were in a quite serious mood but very relaxed and happy to have an extra night in beautiful Paris. After many years of diplomacy and staying abroad, Lenktov was a suitable companion for a lady to spend a night out in Paris with. He decided to take Fenella to a small three-star Michelin restaurant in the Latin Quarter.

It reminded Lenktov of a restaurant called Le Pavillion in New York, just off the intersection with Park Avenue and Fifty Seventh Street. Tonkin had invited him and the Greek Papadakis to dinner there a few years ago. Lenktov had been impressed by Tonkin's hospitality. For a moment he thought about ordering a bottle of Petrus '52, as 'onkin had done, but changed his mind and asked for a bottle of his favorite Burgundy - 1usigny '61.

Fenella was moved by the distinctive French atmosphere and enjoyed the wine nd food. She put her hand over Lenktov's and looked at him with a smile on her face. - I think this is far more than I deserve Nika!"

Lenktov put the other hand over hers and stroked it gently. -"Nonsense! :veryone deserves a small break from time to time! Tomorrow we will be caught in the niddle of a game that could result in our death, so we certainly deserve an evening out", ιe said and looked at her fondly.

Fenella bent forward, and kissed him onthe open palm. - "Thank you!" She miled vigilantly and lovingly at him. In the distance, they could hear soft music playing ιt the deck of one of the tourist boats that slipped past the Notre Dame towards the ;eine.

Late in the afternoon the following day, October 29, Fenella arrived at the KNA ιotel in Stavanger, Norway. The taxi driver carried her two suitcases into the lobby. She hecked in with a Belgian passport, registered her last residence in Brussels and her ιirthplace in Ghent.

The next day she left for Bergen and stayed until the end of the week in the hotel Jeptun under a different name. The hotel was full of German officers and youth from he Ubootlehrgroup who practiced at the dive tank at the NATO base of Haakonsvern ust outside the city.

Chapter 5

THE KEY
Flensburg - Berlin - New York, October 1970

It was quite crowded at café Uhse in Flensburg at night. Sailors, shipyard workers, navy employees, business people and bar flies, many of them female. The place was a gold mine for Tonkin's activities and among the safest channels for information and new contacts.

Two of his most trusted informants sat with him in his regular stall. They were young ladies, originally from Eastern Germany. The German locksmith, who had delivered the key to Watson at the café, stayed on after Phil Young had left and eventually became quite tipsy.
"Five hundred German Marks for a small job is not a daily affair", he thought to himself. He lifted his glass towards Watson, who sat in the other end of the room. - "He is probably American. At least, the key I made for him had the letters US engraved on it.
- "Marine Man! I was in the navy myself", he said proudly as he laid his arm on the shoulder of the woman sitting beside him.
- "Five hundred Marks! They have a lot of money over there. No wonder we lost the war." The woman let go for a moment and went to the bathroom. She passed Watson and walked in the hallway where the telephone was, calling and exchanging some words with the person on the other end. When she returned to the room, Watson had already gone. She sat down and put her arm around the locksmith who was obviously in an excellent mood.

Tonkin sat in the car in the parking lot outside the café, for another hour and a half before the woman came to support the locksmith and led him to his van. She waved him as he drove away and then returned back inside the bar.

Tonkin started the engine and followed the car. The van took off from the main road south of the city and followed the coastal road further south. He soon turned onto a side road, away from the buildings and stopped just off the seafront.

Tonkin turned onto the side of the road with the light turned off and saw that the locksmith almost fell out of the car and went down to the beach. He stumbled upon opening the zipper in his trousers as Tonkin grabbed his neck and pushed his face down into the water. Tonkin held his head under water with a firm grip over the neck until the man no longer moved. After that he went back to the car and continued along the coastal road and further onto the highway south to Hamburg.

Two days later the Flensburger Zeitung reported that a middle-aged man had been found dead just south of Flensburg. The cause of death was drowning, but there was nothing to suggest foul play. The man had been a blacksmith and a locksmith and owned a workshop in Flensburg. The article was printed on the same page as a report about the USS A1's fleet visit.

Phil sat in the hall and read the two stories. He thought for a moment about the key and read the article again before shrugging his shoulders and reading on. - "Hardly any connection with our case", he said to himself.

The local police considered the drowning and alcohol prophylaxis in the blood of the deceased in addition to the fact that the zipper of his pants was open, as a typical case they knew from previous drowning accidents.

The door in the van was open, and nothing, neither the two hundred marks in the wallet, nor the equipment in the car had been stolen. A soap bar was found in one of his pockets, with an imprint of a key, partially washed away by the water. There was an inscription on the imprint that they guessed had read "US 4". The grooves had mostly vanished.

The investigator dutifully sent the soap to the surveillance service with questions and asked if they had any comment. It was assumed that the key might be from the post-war period and that the blacksmith would have copied it for someone. The workshop didn't have any register or order book so there were no further explanations to be found.

For the sake of routine, because of the high military activity in the area and since the inscription resembled the letters "US", a photo was sent to the US Embassy. The CIA representative in Berlin received the report and the photo without noticing anything of that woke his curiosity. However, as the information was related to a sudden death, it was standard protocol to forward the information to headquarters.

Thanks to the fact that he had shown a high level of activity, for example, by calling Zana and Tonkin in Berlin, Conahan quickly aquired the report. With his innate skepticism to coincidences and turmoil over Tonkin's movements, he immediately became interested in the matter. However, this was not until the end of October after the A1 left Flensburg. He had drawn an assumed profile of the whole key, probably about 3 cm long, and asked the technical department at the Navy Museum to investigate if a similar design was used earlier. The answer came back promptly:

"The key shape and marking were standard in most of the navy vessels and used in most of today's operational ships. The manufacturer is requested, but the digit "4" did not provide a guideline other than that the key was probably delivered to a vessel built between 1967 - 68 ".

Conahan asked the Berlin office to get a list of all US navy vessels that had arrived in northern Germany in the last year. The list came after a few days, but this time from the Navy headquarters, with both call and departure dates imposed. Only four of the vessels were from the relevant period and had come to Hamburg and Bremerhafen in February and May. All were lighter surface vessels without special operational missions. Conahan saw no significant connection between these calls and the incident in Flensburg. He set the case aside and asked the dutiful navy to check if any of the four keys on board were missing.

Three days later, however, at the beginning of November, a new list came in response to the inquiry, directly from Berlin, following a task from the German port authorities.

Again, Conahan put the list away, but intuitively took it back again. - "I knew it, I knew it! There were only naval vessels and no submarines on the other list!" He quickly flipped through and stopped his finger at Flensburg. The USS A1 had been at the Warneman workshop for a week. A phone to the US submarine headquarters confirmed that the ship was built in 1968. - "There we have it"!

Conahan pulled up the chair and grabbed the phone receiver again. The A1 had left Flensburg six days ago and was already in international waters under operational command. Contact with the ship was only for those with a special clearance.

Through an old friend and submarine captain, he was able to obtain the list of the names of the crew and officers on board after much persuasion. His contact at the Naval Museum, confirmed that all keys on the A1 were marked "US" and in series starting with 4, 5, 6 or 7.

Although he had a feeling that it would not be possible to find those responsible for stealing the key, Conahan was no longer in doubt that the events in Flensburg were somehow a part of a bigger picture. - "There is no doubt that we have a case", he sighed in relief, before gathering the team that already knew of Tonkin's travels, together with his unknown female companion.

Everyone was given a list of names of the crew aboard the A1 to review what they could gather from personal data. They were to crosscheck criminal records and find out if there were family ties within Europe, with particular emphasis on any connections relating to West Germany.

USSR Vostok - November 1970

Captain Voltov breathed out the last days of frustration before he gave orders to his crew. - "Direction north-west, at 6 knots – 90 feet deep". He had received orders from navy command that his submarine, the USSR Vostok was to follow the US A1 submarine, out of Danish waters.

They had no trouble reading the signals and the messages indicating that the A1 was on the move from Flensburg in a surface position. The USSR Vostok, quiet as a mouse, followed its larger, more advanced, older American sister, without being noticed.

Once out of Danish waters, he had orders to return east to a new destination just outside Stockholm. Besides that, Voltov did not have any specific information concerning the mission and felt a certain discomfort considering previous risky landing assignments in the Stockholm Archipelago. He shook his head to physically get rid of his thoughts.

The Russian navy was largely familiar with the Swedish security zones and mining patterns. Partly because the Swedes themselves had provided the Russians with information in order to prevent complications in the area; and partly because Russian agents had been working to uncover the Swedish security systems for a few years.

Voltov went to his favorite place in the map room and followed the A1 movements in detail. Suddenly, as the ferry to Sweden passed between the two submarines, the signals from A1 disappeared. Captain Janson, who was fully aware of the Russians lingering at their tail, used the opportunity to dive rapidly below 90 feet deep; the depth at which Vostok had chosen to follow the A1.

Tonkin didn't know if he, by a random communication error, had just avoided being blown in the neck by Conahan. He stayed in northern Germany for one week after the A1 had left Flensburg on October 27. Watson and Gerber performed control checks for the imming tanks as the ship was being repaired in the shipyard. The equipment was ready for assembly in Bergen by 14 November, when the A1 contacted Haakonsvern. enktov was already in place as an attaché at the embassy in Oslo.

Tonkin had deliberately avoided contacting his people in Berlin and was still laying tourist at the little seaside cabin by the coast. He set up a meeting in Hamburg ith one of Tass' agents to acquire updated information from Stasi and Moscow.

That afternoon, at the time Conahan was having his meeting to go through the st of names, Tonkin received a packet folded in a newspaper, handed to him at the orner of Herbertstrasse. It contained papers with coded information and a key to a ntal apartment in the Hamburg city centre. Arriving at the apartment, he sat down to ecode the messages. After an hour of concentration he finally had an overview.

He had information from an agent in Bremerhafen, stating that Interpol in Berlin ad asked to receive a list of all US Navy vessels that had visited ports in northern ermany in the past months. Furthermore, through the message from Moscow, he had arned that the CIA had been making inquires about his travels together with a female avel companion. Tonkin intuitively knew that this was nothing more than normal CIA ivolvement. He closed his eyes and pictured the brave, broad-shouldered CIA staff om that time in Bonn.

"Conahan! It must be Conahan", he shouted before jumping out of the chair as he rew the crumpled paper on the floor. However, he quickly regained self control and ought through the situation.

If Conahan had traced him to the Flensburg area and at the same time coupled it ith simultaneous calls by naval vessels, he probably already had the impression that e A1 could have some meaning.

On the other hand he found it quite incomprehensible how the CIA could connect im with a woman travel companion. The only event Tonkin came up with was the short rive with Fenella back to the hotel in Como. As there were no other possibilities to hoose from, Conahan should have known one way or another that he had been in omo. Tromboli must have been out late so that the local agent at the hotel had received is information on time. Or someone had informed, which he greatly doubted. But enella, who had no known identity in Italy, could not be recognized or known to the mericans. He was sure that Fenella's identity had not been revealed, nor the fact that e was in Norway under a different identity. The information provided by the CIA was lso marked with all recipient sites and none of these were in Scandinavia. It was uggested that the search was a wild guess and that they had no idea whatsoever about hat was about to happen.

Tonkin was nevertheless most concerned about what Conahan could discover in is own "backyard". He found it likely that he had already have discovered a link to A1. - Hopefully it will take him a long time to discover the relationship between Kelly and e brother", he thought to himself. - "Not to mention the connection to the KGB", he dded. He felt they had covered their tracks pretty well, so he was not too worried. After ll he knew how complex and time-consuming intelligence work was.

He suddenly realized that his shirt was soaked in sweat so he stood up and eaded towards the shower. On his way into the shower, he decided to alert New York to alculate a certain risk and possibly take precautions.

There was no time to lose, and Tonkin found it necessary to break the rules to otify Fenella, who was now in Bergen. The following morning, on November 4, a message was sent via Oslo to Lippke in the mountains. He gave the message to Fenella later that day, during their regular meeting.

When Fenella was back in the hotel, she opened the envelope and decoded the message. She was asked to take extra care and told to fly to Trondheim two days later on a flight that landed at 14:05. Tonkin would meet her at Værnes airport. He told her to book a return trip via Oslo to Stavanger with a new identity and stay there for the rest of the week before returning to Bergen.

Fenella found the letter very disturbing. However, she estimated that plans had not changed since Tonkin told her to return to Bergen on time. She stayed up late wondering what might have happened.

That same evening, Tonkin received a new passport under the name of Heinz Zneider, supposedly a German mining engineer. He then boarded a ferry to Sweden and was picked up at the pier upon arrival at Værmdø in Stockholm and driven to a bus stop where he took a bus to Østersund. From there he went to Storlien, crossing via Meråker to Stjørdal in Norway. Tromboli and Zana were to pick him up at the stop in Hell, north of Trondheim from where they would drive to Værnes and pick up Lenktov and Fenella. Even if Tonkin felt tired, he felt satisfied as he sat in the bus on his way to Norway.

"Conahan would probably be very pleased if his own people had shown such determination", he said to himself. "Actually, the Americans are idiots. They have no chance at figuring out my well thought out intelligence system". He fell asleep, with a smile of content on his face.

Lenktov had already been in place at the embassy in Oslo for a week. The Ministry of Foreign Affairs had been informed in advance about the transfer and the arrival of a new attaché, focusing on social affairs and economy. At the hotel Altona in Paris he had said goodbye to Fenella, who, after checking out of the Calais hotel the same day, had travelled to Stavanger under the name of Vera Schlosseneck.

The message from Tonkin about coming to Trondheim had been quite secret, but Lenktov felt he had to travel without following the standard protocol of notifying the Norwegian authorities of his travels. He wanted to avoid being followed or spotted by POT in Trondheim.

He was cautious even if he suspected that POT did not have a file on him yet. After all he had just been to the embassy for a week and Norwegian bureaucracy was usually quite slow when it came to processing and updating information on staff changes at the embassy. But right now, it was paramount to ensure that the operation continued as planned, so he would be extremely careful.

Chapter 6

THE PLAN
Trondheim, November 1970

"Heinz Zneider" got out at the back of the dirty bus, carrying a briefcase. He walked through the crowded bus stop at Hell and followed the directions towards the taxis. He found Tromboli's caravan that was parked close by. Zana pushed the back door aside and let him in.

Tonkin wiped off his coat and let out a sight. So far everything had worked out. During the bus tour, he had thought about how much information was necessary to share with the tree of them. He had reached the conclusion that too much information could easily disturb them. Both Tromboli and Zana were curious and wanted to know what would happen. Tonkin asked them to wait until they had gotten Lenktov and Fenella.

Tromboli told Tonkin how their trip had gone so far. They reached Værnæs after a short drive and caught sight of Lenktov who stood at the edge of a parking lot, reading a newspaper. Tonkin asked Tromboli to drive around to make sure Lenktov had not been followed.

A short while later they parked just behind Lenktov, who had already observed Tromboli at the steering wheel as the car passed the first time. He strolled to the car and did not notice Zana and Tonkin before the back door with the dark sunscreen windows was pushed up and he got in.

Fenella's plane landed at 02:05 p.m. She had been allowed to bring both of her suitcases into the cabin so she did not have to wait for the luggage. Behind dark sunglasses, she threw a trained look over at the people who waited at the passenger exit without seeing anything suspicious.

Zana greeted her with a friendly embrace at the arrivals hall, just like a relative would do. She took one of her suitcases and they walked to the car. Fenella sat in front with Tromboli, gave Tonkin a smile and nodded to Lenktov. Tonkin told Tonkin to drive north towards Verdal where they stopped on a small side road.

All of them sat in the car, facing each other. "First, I'd like to say that nothing has gone wrong so far. Everything should go according to plan and we will make only minor changes if it becomes necessary". Tonkin said as he studied their faces.

Zana lit a cigarette and then said, - "We were a little worried about the message, of course, but this sounds good. Why would you still meet us here?"

"Primarily to make sure that we have a plan if something goes wrong". Tonkin looked at each of them before he continued, - "The CIA seems to suspect that something is going on. I received information that they observed me, and possibly a woman, in Germany and elsewhere on the continent. Currently, we must conclude that they know nothing. But they did collect information on all US-navy ship calls to northern Germany in the last few months. There may be a correlation with A1, but we do not think the Americans have any more than that. He looked at Fenella.

- "We are pretty sure that there is no thread that would lead to Kelly". Lenktov squeezed his chin between his thumb and forefinger. -"But we need to set up an additional safety net. We are about to take chances we should really avoid. If we are observed in some way together, it would be hard to carry out our mission". Tonkin suddenly scratched the back of his shoulder while talking. He was clearly irritated. - "We are pretty sure that nobody has been following us so far", said Tromboli. - "If we continue in the same way we shouldn't have a problem".

- "Ok", said Fenella, "we have no problem yet, but we must make sure we can handle the situation if we get into trouble later".

- "Quite right", Tonkin answered a little bit more comfortably. - "There is no doubt that we must now secure two courier outlets from Bergen. Originally the plan was that Tromboli and Zana picked up the package and then headed north with the coastal passenger ship "Hurtigruten", but that is no longer viable as the only alternative".

He turned to Lenktov. - "First, you have to go with Zana and Tromboli to Bergen" Lenktov looked confused.

- "That means I have to travel back to Oslo with your flight ticket and in your name" continued Tonkin, "And thus the Embassy should be safe to report back in your name There are hardly any problems with it".

- "Fenella stays here in the Trondheim area for a few days and returns via Oslo to Stavanger, where she stays for a week before Bergen". He nodded towards Fenella.

- "Remember to change hotels as we talked about and avoid using the same identity" She nodded back but felt the usual discomfort by receiving orders from Tonkin.

- "But how does Lenktov get out if Zana and I take the car on the expressway north?" Tromboli asked. - "After all, he is a registered diplomat!"

- "Listen!" Tonkin raised both his hands to get their full attention. - "As we planned, you should bring the "package" from Fenella and bring it north to Tromsø via Hurtigruten From there, Zana will take the car over to Finland and Sweden and south again while you enter the Soviet Union via Finland. And Fenella, after erasing anything that could be traced to her, flies back to Geneva with a whole new identity".

He nodded towards Tromboli. - "Zana travels with you on Hurtigruten, partly as planned, but both under new identity and without a car. At the same time, Lenktov and Fenella take over their identities and travel eastwards by car. Of course, we do not make any changes to the "package" still being brought north along the coast by you and across the border to Russia. But instead of leaving the route from Tromsø via Skibotn to Kilpisjærvi in Finland, Tromboli travels all the way north to Kirkenes and Bjørnevatn and then crosses the border directly into Russia."

He stopped for a moment and thought about the controversial plans earlier in the year between the leadership in Moscow and the Finnish president about a possible Russian acquisition of northern Finland. He then continued, - "He has done it several times before, and we do not expect any problems". He looked at Tromboli, - "You get all the information in Tromsø and Kirkenes. Our people have already arranged accommodation and transportation. You are going out via Boris Gleb and on to Nikel and Moscow," Tromboli nodded and smiled sharply.

Tonkin continued, -"It is important that we keep the transfer plan at the Bergen meeting place, not at least in view of possible tensions or pure coincidences. Watson and Gerber will stay at the hotel Neptune from November 10 until they leave Bergen on November 23. Watson goes to Copenhagen by plane from Flesland via Stavanger and Gerber by truck to Kristiansand and then further by ferry. That same week, there will be about 30 German submarine cadets in the hotel, all of which are going to be training in the dive tank at Haakonsvern. Of course, it fits perfectly into the operation. However, they leave Friday, and only our people will stay there until Sunday and someone else possibly longer". Tonkin took a break and nodded to the others.

- "To prevent something from appearing suspicious, we still have to make Fenella arrive at the meeting place on Monday, November 23 on her own, and have Lenktov and Zana follow later, both in turquoise as two joggers on a training trip through the valley. Tromboli takes a taxi directly to the pier from Scandia Hotel and waits for Zana to arrive. After retrieving the package from Fenella, Zana leaves the valley on her own and preferably takes the local bus which passes the end of the valley every fifteen minutes, back to the center. Lenktov and Fenella then take over the role of joggers and go down to the car from the meeting point sometime after Zana has left and immediately drive eastwards out of Bergen towards Geilo". He stretched out his hands.

- "Simple, isn't it"? He said with a smile on his face. - "We are therefore sure that those of you who are best known along the coast, travel that way, while it is relatively quick and uncomplicated for Lenktov and Fenella to get out of the country by car via Geilo. It would be far too big a risk to take if Lenktov was sitting on Hurtigruten for days. Fenella could be discovered as well. In any case, if something goes wrong, they will start searching. Because we are so close to the end of the mission, it is now more important than before to make it more difficult for someone to track us. In this way, we avoid having Fenella, even with other identities traced back to a flight out of the country and perhaps further. Like "Tromboli and Zana" on return via Sweden, "Fenella Lorc" will simply be gone! And Nika does not really "exist" in this context!" Tonkin looked triumphantly at them. No one seemed to disagree.

- "Good. First, the problem will be then just to keep Lenktov hidden?" Fenella smiled at Nika who had long imagined various uncomfortable nights in the car with Tromboli on his way to Bergen. - "And I am to go to Tromsø and cross the Finnish border as previously planned, right? But how then, without a car?" Zana looked inquiringly at Tonkin.

- "Of course. As I said, there is no need to change anything more than the change in Bergen. You will be taken care of and helped over the border by my people in northern Norway. They have all the necessary information and are ready to assist you and move you through Skibotn and Helligskogen as soon as you arrive in Tromsø". Tonkin scratched his left shoulder again.

- "What really matters is that the "package" will surely cross the border with Russia near Boris Gleb. You can expect a small patrol waiting to receive you up there!" He gestured towards Tromboli.

- "What about weapons?" Lenktov asked. "We need to be prepared, as it may be necessary, right?"

- "You and Tromboli should have your own German Lugers available, currently hidden in the car now. With the strict Norwegian weapon rules, there is too much security risk if Fenella and Zana are to carry weapons. We should not take that chance". Tonkin looked at Tromboli and turned his head toward Lenktov. - "You make sure he gets his".

They were running out of time, as the Oslo plane would leave in about an hour. Tromboli drove back to Værnes airport. They discussed further details on their way to the airport where Tonkin left them on their way to the plane with his image staring from a perfect passport for embassy clerk Nicolovich Lenktov in his inner pocket. When Lenktov let Tonkin out of the car at the airport, he shook his hand and left a note in his palm stating "Keep an extra eye out for Zana".

Fenella took the airport bus to Hotel Bristol in the Trondheim city center. After checking the room as per her habit, she switched to a room without a balcony and signed in as Vera Jarle for the next three days. Following her plan, she should return to Stavanger on November 9.

hapter 7

RAUD
ew York, November 1970

ergey Kazutin lit a cigarette in the dark alley across the street from Papadakis' partacus restaurant. Half past midnight, he saw Papadakis lock the side door to the estaurant and hurry down the sidewalk. Despite it being late, many people were out alking along the well-lit streets between Broadway and Amsterdam, close to Columbia niversity. Kazutin put out the cigarette, pulled up the zipper on his jacket and stepped to the small newspaper distribution car. He noticed that the Greek walked briskly and eemed quite alert, constantly looking over his sholder.

Tonkin had informed the New York Group through Moscow and Athens, that the IA was likely to shadow Papadakis as a result of intelligence activities in northern urope. Kelly Young's name was not mentioned in the context. Papadakis had been formed and asked to show caution and avoid any intelligence contact. As a result, the reek was terrified and began to behave strangely. The group management concluded ithin two days that they would not risk Papadakis bursting out. There was also a ertain risk that he would contact the CIA. Tonkin's message was graded at the highest vel in Moscow and left no doubt that the matter was important. Kazutin was therefore ut on a mission to make sure that the Greek did not do anything wrong.

Papadakis had seen a movement in the alley across the street. He hurried around e corner and crossed the street to blend in with the people heading towards the bway. He stopped and looked back but didn't see anyone following him. He was a bit ore relaxed as he continued walking towards his apartment on West 113 Street.

After he had entered the apartment building and the receptionist had turned the arm on the front door, he felt safe. He felt relieved when he whistled a tune from Zorba e Greek in the elevator on the way to the 31st floor. Inside the apartment, he gulped a p of whiskey before Kazutin's hand ran right over his neck and struck him unconscious n the floor. Kazutin seized the glass with a slight movement before breaking it on the oor. He went to the bathroom and filled the laundry in one of the marked bags. Then e grabbed the Greek, tipped his shoulder, and walked out in the hallway dragging the ack by the rubber that was firmly tied around the man's left wrist. The door to the undry room was locked and Kazutin pulled the door and the frame loose from the wall nd pushed Papadakis and the bag in and down the laundry chute. He left the frame nd the door on the floor. He then carefully wiped the whiskey glass before leaving the partment with the door unlocked. At the doorstep, he picked up the pile of the New ork Herald newspapers and put on his paperboy cap before he took the elevator down the garage in the basement. A quick peek into the laundry room showed that no one ad thrown clothes in it before Papadakis had hit the steel floor in the collection ontainer. Kazutin drove to the gate and he pressed the opener. He then pushed the eaker button and told the guard that the "newspaper round was over".

ate in the afternoon of November 10, Spartacus's chief accountant reported to the olice that Papadakis had disappeared and was probably exposed to something criminal ecause his apartment was open and unlocked.

Sometime later, the laundry agency reported that a person was found to have perished in the laundry collection in one of their cars. Because the Greek was registered with both American and Greek nationalities, the FBI was notified. Their file on the man showed comments from the CIA and they therefore chose to follow the investigation themselves.

Apparently, the man was most likely drunk when he planned to throw the laundry down the cute. Somehow, he seemed to have gotten into trouble with the bag hooked around his wrist. To loosen it up he most likely took off the door and the frame with the result that he himself had fallen down the laundry chute. In practice, this could not be possible. The investigators found no special traces of anything in the apartment indicating that others might have been there, except perhaps from the whiskey that was spilled over the floor, but probably suggested that the man had not been sober. It was concluded that the cause of the death was a self-inflicted accident. However, in the report to the CIA it was noted that it was strange that the whiskey glass had no fingerprints.

Conahan, who was already searching for the German A1 case in America, had immediate interest in the event, primarily because Papadakis was listed as a possible contact for the East German STASI. - "Check his background and send people to the restaurant". He looked at the two agents.
- "And take a night out with the guys in Athens. You will find out something. In addition I have to much experience to believe the explanation the Agency has on this matter".
- "And make sure that you check all data and people against the registrars and people on the A1!" Conahan leaned against the heavy office chair and closed his eyes the way he used to. With his right hand, he rubbed the wrinkles over his forehead back and forth.
- "If we find a connection here, it must mean that the KGB has liquidated the guy out of fear of something. If that turns out to be the case, they are likely to regret it. We'd hardly cared about the guy if it was not for his death", he thought to himself.

The thirteen staff members in the restaurant were questioned one by one over the next two days. All of them were asked to provide their home address and information on their education, previous employment, travel and places of residence in the last year.

The information obtained was then compared to population records and checked to see if the police and intelligence had files on any of them. It turned out that two of the waiters and one of the cooks didn't have legal residence permits. Two of these had arrived with Turkish nationality, but were both Kurds. The third had arrived via London to the United States as a British citizen, but residence permit was expired.

A request to Scotland Yard showed that the woman was not British but a Somali citizen and that she had not received an asylum application for permanent residence in England. She had obtained fake papers and arrived in the United States before the application was finished and for that reason noted as missing or in hiding.
Conahan doubted if any of these could have anything to do with his case. None of the three had left New York the whole year. Only two of the younger women in the restaurant, both of which American citizens, went to school, had graduated or been abroad during the past year. One of them had taken summer courses in Switzerland and the other had completed a year's cooking education in Italy. For the record, he asked Interpol in Paris to inspect the circles and friends they had had during their stay abroad.

The feedback brought little new, except that the school in Switzerland thought that Kelly Young, had excelled as an extraordinarily experienced and knowledgeable student. She had not kept in contact with her teachers or fellow students, except one from Iceland.

Conahan had an immediate reaction when he heard Iceland. He knew that the US military base there was the supply station for parts of the Atlantic fleet, including the submarines. A phone call to the boss and a subsequent reply, confirmed that Brit Jonsdottir was known by the Icelandic E-service, but by no means other than her name in a file of supervised persons. The file was not her own but belonged to the leader of the Icelandic Communist Party, who had listed her name on a member list of Young Pioneers. At the bottom of the fax from the boss, it was said that Miss Jonsdottir had been an exchange student at the University of Columbia a few years earlier. Her home address in New York was listed as c/o Young, in Greenwich Village. Conahan caressed his upper arm thoughtfully. - "Hm", he said to himself. - "Well, we have to check in any case". He decided to talk to this Kelly Young.

Trondheim, November 1970

Lenktov was very concerned about the piece of paper he had received from Tonkin. Although he felt that this was barely a general precaution, he knew that Tonkin had to have a good reason to ask him to take care.

The Volkswagen headed south from Værnes Airport, with him, Zana and Trompoli onboard. They had decided to travel a short distance south and spend the time doing holiday things before moving on to Bergen. About 10 kilometers south of Trondheim towards Klett was a large campsite with a lot of rental cabins that were frequented even this late in the autumn. Tromboli spoke a little Norwegian and arranged for two cabins for them, one for himself and Zana and the other for Lenktov. They decided to stay there for a few days and take short trips into Trondheim and the surrounding area.

Lenktov, who had realized that something was wrong, kept a close eye on Zana. He offered to accompany her to a trade show in Trondheim the following day. She could drive the carand they could both use their new identities.

The meeting with Tonkin had almost meant that Zana had to change her role in the operation. She had long thought that this might be her only opportunity to get enough money for a new life in the United States. She did not doubt that Conahan would appreciate being able to help the Russians again. She thought for a moment about what Tonkin had said earlier about the Americans seeing him together with a woman. She wandered whether Conahan knew that it was she. She was worried that Lenktov was supposed to join her and Tromboli on their way south, but, because the plans for the retrieval and delivery of the "package", or the film, were not changed, it played a very minor role. The most important thing for her in the days to come was to get in touch with Conahan just at the right time and that she really would manage to carry out an unnoticed exchange. If she contacted Conahan prematurely, it would cause a significant risk that the case could leak and that the Russians might realize that something was wrong. She could even put herself at risk of being exposed and worst of all liquidated. Nevertheless, when it came to the exchange, she would have a lot of time to change the film on the way from the meeting place in Isdalen valley outside Bergen or the bus to the city center before meeting Tromboli on the boat.

It all depended, in any case, on obtaining a film roll of the same type that would be used on board the A1. She had long thought about what Tonkin's plan could be. It would obviously be too risky to smuggle a camera on board the A1. The simplest would be to let one of the crew take pictures of what was desired and then smuggle the film out of the boat. The crew on American submarines had hardly any cameras other than the usual 35 mm. But undoubtedly a film with very high light sensitivity was needed, as it would not be possible to use flash below deck without the risk of being detected. Watson or Gerber would probably have brought the film on land and to Fenella. She had no choice but to gamble that the film was 35mm and to get a copy herself. Which should be easy during the morning in Trondheim!

Before leaving Værnes, Lenktov had agreed with Fenella that they would meet outside the entrance to Nidaros Cathedral at 16:00 in the afternoon if necessary and if she had anything new to announce.

Zana was obviously relieved when Lenktov finally offered to accompany her on the shopping trip. They parked the car in Olavsplassen in the city center and walked past the shops down to Ravnkloa by the harbor.

Zana was surprised to find some European fashion items in this "ice-ocean metropolis". The summer clothes were on offer as it was already fall and purchasing these beautiful clothes already gave her a glimpse of the escape she would have from this cold in just a matter of weeks.

She did not intend to throw her life away for anything less than real luxury and the thoughts flashed through her mind as she let the skirts slip between her fingers. No more old and fat vodka drinking mood-less Russians! America was the country of her future. South Africa has a long tradition of double agents, she thought to herself. - "Most ended up on the American side."

Suddenly she woke up and shook off her dreams. She was standing suspiciously between two shelves while one of the ladies in the shop politely shook her by her elbow and worriedly asked if anything was wrong. Zana quickly became aware. For a short moment, she felt the trembling drag of fear along her back before she was on top of the situation again and smiled and thanked the woman before she left the store.

Lenktov sat waiting at a café close by and she realized that the most important thing about the city tour, namely buying film to bring to Bergen, had to be arranged. Just up the street was a bookshop with a Kodak sign outside. Zana turned and looked over at the café and saw Lenktov sitting there. She decided to make the film purchase now while she had the opportunity. The woman behind the counter was nice and helpful and spoke good English. Zana told her what kind of film she wanted, and asked for two rolls, just in case.

Lenktov had a good view over the street so he could see when Zana came out of the clothing store and walk over towards the bookstore. He got up and left the café just as she turned the corner on the opposite side of the road. As she entered the bookstore, he was able to get a good view into the store. He saw that Zana requested something special and that the shopkeeper picked up the two rolls of film and handed them to her. He immediately pulled back and hurried quickly across the street and around the corner where, through the corner window, he could see Zana coming straight towards him from across the street. He quickly returned to the café and ordered a second cup of coffee as Zana entered the door. Without showing signs of the turmoil he felt, he smiled and said,

- "Great, finally you're back. And you found something?" He nodded toward the bags of clothes that Zana had with her. - "Yes and it is absolutely amazing how cheap you can get some clothes now after the season", she lit up and pulled out a pink light beach dress. - "I really look forward to using this one as we go back to the warm weather soon", Zada added contently.

Lenktov thought to himself that the expression really was quite symbolic. She would hardly go back to a warmer climate after what he had just seen. In fact quite on the contrary. He did not say a word about the film by Lenktov, knew she had no camera. Back at the campsite later in the day, she did not say anything to Tromboli about the film and had obviously not been commissioned by him to buy it.

They decided to end the city tour and at the same time go to the meeting with Fenella at the church at 4:00 p.m. A few minutes earlier, they saw Fenella walking through the door of the open cathedral alone and followed her while at the same time showed apparent great interest in the beautifully decorated church. Lenktov passed Fenella, who showed by shaking her head that she had nothing new to tell. Zana stood further back in the church and studied the story of King Olav the Holy. He walked closer to Fenella and let the note he had written in the cafe slip unnoticed into her hand in her left pocket of the hoodie. Then he continued inside the church and sat down in front of the altar. Fenella went out and passed Zana without acknowledging her. Back in the hotel room at Bristol she opened the paper and read the Russian text:

"Z irregularity. Something wrong. Keep control".

Fenella immediately wrote a message, left the hotel again and went into the shopping center close by, where she handed over the coded message to Tonkin's contact person, who then forwarded the message to the embassy in Oslo that same evening.

New York, November 1970

Kelly Young was in shock after Papadakis was found dead. She had no doubt that he had been murdered in cold blood after seeing how clearly frightened and uneasy he had been in the last few days. Following the interrogations with the FBI, she was very worried that they might connect the dots between the murder, her trip to Europe, and at worst of all - Phil. She considered whether to contact Tonkin but then realized that he had already been informed of what had happened.

The restaurant manager also received a new request from the FBI for more information and inquiries. Kelly was terrified, because she did not understand the KGB's role in the matter. It was hard to believe that it was the FBI or American intelligence that had killed Papadakis. For a moment she considered fleeing, maybe back to the Middle East, but decided to stay.

One day, Kelly was presented to a difficult "CIA-like" agent who smiled broadly and called himself Conahan. - "We would like to have a little chat with you, Miss, it will not take a long time", he said to her politely.

Kelly was reassured by the kind tone and felt she might have exaggerated the fear of being discovered. - "We can have a seat over here", He showed her into the room and pointed to a chair.

- "How long have you been working in this restaurant, Miss?" he asked her.

- "About one year", Kelly replied.

- "I saw you have been in Switzerland, too? Good school?" he continued.

- "Yes, excellent, Papadakis paid for it. He was just amazing", she replied and looked sadly at Conahan who continued,

- "You had a friend from Iceland at school? Have you been to Iceland? By the way, they have a huge American military base there!"

Kelly felt her heart beating and was sure that Conahan could hear and see it. There was more to this "innocent" interview than she had thought. Brit, did they know about Brit? She calmed herself and was happy that the light had been faded down in the restaurant. She became unsure, and thought that maybe Conahan only knew the name from Switzerland and had not investigated Brit. But they certainly knew she had been in Lebanon as well. She decided to take a shot.

- "Yes", she replied, it was Brit "I was on exchange in Lebanon in 1967 and met her for the first time there. But I have not had contact with her after Switzerland and unfortunately, I have never seen Iceland, no"! She smiled apologetically.

Conahan's face didn't reveal any expression, but he was very surprised to "strike at the core" since Kelly had avoided telling him that the same Brit had lived with them the year she went to Columbia University. It worried him and told him that they were on the right track. This was undoubtedly an experienced and intelligent girl who would not let anything slip, even under pressure. He decided to play the game further in the hopes of revealing something. He would contact the intelligence service to acquire more detailed information.

- "Well, that's it", he said smiling as he thanked Kelly for the talk and apologized for the inconvenience. She stood up and nodded back before continuing with her work in the restaurant.

At Langley, a telex from the Secret Service contained a response to Conahan's request to check for possible affiliations between the A1's personnel and the 13 employees in the restaurant:

Att: Conahan
"4 persons at the restaurant have the same surname as personnel affiliated with the A1. Two female (f) and two male (m).
1. John Hanson m. - List E. Hanson f. - P. Hanson m.
2. Jim Johnson m. - O. Johnson.m
3. Phil Young m. - K. Young. f
4. Ron Gilford m. - M. Gilford. f
In total, about 250-300 names were cross checked. The two crews were 120 each in addition to spouses if they had another last name.

The telex was copied and the original was filed in Conahan's file in New York. A copy was sent to the FBI in New York.

At about the same time, another telegram to Conahan was delivered to Langley's eception and received by the guard. The telegram was sent from a place in Norway alled Hetris Kristiansund, and read:

"Will call on Friday a.m. Norwegian time. Zana".

.elly had already decided to leave when she returned back home from work. She called 1e student's travel agency, got a ticket to Paris that evening and collected what she eeded of money and cards, including two French prepaid cards that Tonkin had rovided her for emergency use. In her passport with her own picture, the name was 'rit Jonsdottir from Iceland, who was supposedly returning home after having been a tudent in the United States.

Two days later Kelly unpacked her little suitcase in a small room overlooking the 1shionable hotel Beur au Lac in Zurich, Switzerland. Since she was still uncertain about 1e role of the KGB in the matter, she chose to remain silent and go "underground" for 1e time being. The CIA never found out where she went and she never returned to her arents' home in New York.

Back in Langley the next day, Conahan was furious as a tiger behind the walls of is office when he heard about Kelly's disappearance. He kicked the office chair as if it 'ere a feather and cursed before it hit the wall with a bang that could be heard around 1e building.

"Bloody idiots, no check at the airports, no photo check, no control at all!" He 1structed all authorities to search and asked the base in Iceland to immediately get ermission from the police there to arrest Brit Jonsdottir and bring her in for uestioning. He realized that the two telegrams should have been handed over to him in Iew York a year and a half ago, and the rage continued.

"Damn useless CIA shit system!" He shook the papers as if they were to blame. uddenly, however, Phil Young's name came to him from one paper in response to all 1e prayers and his rage was instantly blown away.

"Young!! What the hell? Here we have something!" He got the Secret Service to send 1e file about Phil as a telephoto, and at the same time a secretary to read it aloud over 1e phone.

The register was unclean. The man was a quartermaster, Kelly's brother and his 1ther fought at Pearl Harbor and was a political supporter of Communist haters and the 1cCarthy-friendly President Richard Nixon, etc.

"How in the whole world can a great guy like him support some rusty communist stuff ke that?" Conahan shook his head.

He sent a telex to the Naval Headquarters, describing the situation and stated, - We have reason to believe that a criminal episode in New York can be directly related to 'hil Young aboard the A1. We request that he be withdrawn from service and 1terrogated at Interpol in Scandinavia with his senior officer". The note was dated uesday, November 17, 1970.

The answer did not arrive until two days later, November 19 at 12:00 a.m:

"A1 is in open sea under its own command. The shore command has been notified but there is no comment is of yet".

The message was signed by the Submarine Admiralty secretary. He put the copy of hi message aside and instead studied the message from Zana. - "Finally, she make contact!"

It meant that she had something to tell him, while at the same time confirmin; that she was involved in an operation in Scandinavia, probably regarding the A1.

He sat down and summed everything up. - "We had the case with Tonkin and th woman in Como and probably London. Probably Zana. Both have disappeared. W followed the key issue from the A1 in Flensburg to Norway and over here via Iceland an Kelly and Phil and a Greek killed by the KGB".

The KGB, Tonkin, Zana and Norway. Conahan counted on his fingers. Four. Th little finger was pointing up in the air. - "What are you hiding little friend?" He looke sharply at the last finger. There was little he could do for now, other than wait for th phone call from Zana on Thursday. The central station was told that all incoming call that day should be transferred to his nearest phone wherever he stayed. He decided n to take the risk of asking the Norwegian police to trace the woman in Kristiansund, fo fear of spoiling the matter.

The telegraph office in Kristiansund, Norway, had paid and expedited th telegram from Zana. She was quite relieved when it was done, and quite sure no one ha noticed it. Lenktov and Tromboli were busy at a gas station, about to switch to winte tires on the car. She expected they would arrive in Bergen on Friday morning, Novembe 20 and that there would be no problem finding a suitable phone. She had time unt evening because of the time difference. She looked forward to talking to Conahan wh she imagined to be both stressed and relieved. She was convinced that he would bot scream and shout at her.

Chapter 8

NATO Base HAAKONSVERN

Saturday morning, November 14 at 6.00 a.m. the A1 slid into partial surface position north of the Hellesøy lighthouse. It continued south through the overwhelming landscape, heading into the fjord that hosted the Nato base at Haakonsvern outside Bergen in Norway.

Two Norwegian motor torpedo boats accompanied the A1. By 7 o'clock, the fog lingering over the blue calm fjord started to disappear in the morning light. Commander Jansson made sure the 186 Meter long A1 arrived safely at its destination. The guard on the base was sharpened and the sheltered location was such that it hardly represented any security problem for the repair along the dock. A unit of Norwegian air defense stationed a few kilometers away was also in position for security reasons.

The Embassy and NATO had made agreements with the US Department of Defense regarding on-board visits while the submarine was being repaired. Representatives from research institutions and Norwegian and foreign naval units were to arrive and one of them was a whole delegation from the nuclear energy institute at Kjeller in eastern Norway.

Watson and Gerber arrived at hotel Neptun in downtown Bergen later that day. After having parked the car in the hotel garage and checked into their rooms, they decided to take a trip to the city. The job at the base would not start until on Monday morning when the truck with the equipment was in place. Watson knew that Fenella would arrive in Bergen only later this week. He had no idea of her current whereabouts.

Early in the night, they returned to the small bar of the hotel together with a handful of German future submarines were trained at the diving facilities at Haakonsvern. Gerber praised his own excellence and that they had him, and thanked the navy for the submarines in operation. The young aspirants were very aware when Gerber talked about the big American nuclear submarines he had been on board. Watson remained wisely at a distance and failed to attend their discussion. .

On Monday morning, November 9th Fenella was ready for travel in Trondheim and a few hours later she disappeared from Værnes Airport during the 12day trip to Oslo and Stavanger. The tickets were purchased in a different name than she had used at the hotel in Trondheim. The patch from Lenktov made her extra troubled and more careful than she would normally be. It was impossible for now to know if Zana had had any contact with others and if she had already been watched. She pulled herself back into the airplane seat and unconsciously took a quick overview of the passengers in the seats behind. Several of them stared back and Fenella was drawn back to reality. She got angry with herself thinking that it was all silly and overreacting. Early in the afternoon, she went from the plane into the arrivals hall at Sola Airport in Stavanger, picked up her luggage and continued to the bus. The hotel St. Svithun in Stavanger city center was booked in advance, and she signed in with her correct name for once, Fenella Lorc, Belgian citizen. With the information about Zana fresh in her memory, she made sure that the room had no balcony or access from the outside. The hotel was neutral enough, owned by the Inner Mission and known as the "Mission Hotel".

Fenella was eventually easily tired of staying in places that totally lacked culture and content and just was a bedroom. But she had no choice but to kill another week in a place she certainly did not want to be in. In order not to break too much with the environment around her, she still had to behave like she enjoyed the stay and enjoyed herself in Stavanger.

- "Which is almost like wiping dirty camels", she said to herself in Lebanese. She smiled and decided to do some shopping to pass the time as quickly as possible. She felt an inner turmoil after having received the information about Zana. She walked into the nearest shoe store and bought a pair of lightweight rubber boots and an umbrella that were useful in the humid weather.

The Submarine Harbor, Haakonsvern, November 1970

Shortly after breakfast, Gerber and Watson received a phone call about the lorry and equipment on the dock at the A1 at the Marine Base Haakonsvern. They got ready and took an extra look at the equipment in the bags in the car before they left.

Particularly important was the camera that was built into a small oscilloscope that was used for reading and checking voltage values in the ballast tank control panel. The camera was built into a flexible tube with a lens so that the film could be removed by pulling out the front of the instrument at the reading window and then pushing it back in place or by pulling out the entire camera tube with the film in it. It was impossible for anyone to see that the measuring instrument also served as a camera. As they did not know when or what day it was possible to take pictures, of course it was extremely important that the camera was not revealed. Both expected careful inspection at the gates and likely a body search when the Americans were at the dock at the base. The tool bags would therefore remain on board each time they left the area. The film would be brought out as a part of the tool and the oscilloscope when the job was completed.

Both were undoubtedly very excited when they arrived at the checkpoint at the entrance to the base. If any of the operation had already been discovered, they would be aware of it now.

Gerber stared steadily forward and whispered to Watson, - "Condemned! This makes me damn nervous". - "Shut up", Watson hissed between his teeth.

- "Good morning", said the guard from the military police. - "Papers please!" Gerber delivered the papers and ID through the car window and told the guard who they were and what mission they had. The car was waved aside and two additional crews went through the equipment and content check relatively superficially, while they were asked to show their passports and the work sheets. No body search was done.

As expected, none of them had knowledge of the technical tool and the measuring devices found in the car. The camera was obviously not found. After the clearance was completed, a military police car was set to drive in front and follow them to the A1 and the truck.

Watson wiped away sweat on his upper lip, - "Good, this is fine. Nobody has discovered anything since last time". Even Gerber looked more relaxed now.

At the pier, they left the car and went directly onto the A1 road. The military policeman briefed the guard who dropped them at the first deck and sent orders for the officer in charge and the next command, Corbin. He greeted them and smiled immediately when he recognized Gerber and Watson, and thanked them for the last time in Flensburg. With the help of two mariners, they got their own equipment in the car and placed it along the walls of the control room, where the work would mostly take place over the next few days. The oscilloscope bag was placed along the wall just before the captain's door. So far everything had been as planned. - "As expected almost unexpectedly!" Watson thought.

Both, he and Gerber, had experience from visits to military facilities in several places in Europe and had found that the control was poor and primarily aimed at identification.

How they should establish contact with Young was still unclear. Watson would not feel completely safe before he was sure Phil was still on board the submarine. They decided to start getting the new equipment on the truck on board so that it could be pulled out of the area and returned to the yard in Germany. The two in the car had already been in the submarine and found a possible temporary placement opportunity in the torpedo rooms. However, Watson would rather have the equipment in the access area for the repair and at Janson's cabin, so that in some way a barrier was established that could reduce traffic to and from the control room. As the radio room in the hallway between the cabin and the cabinet was not operational on land in the same way as on board, he decided to take the opportunity to put the equipment there. Everyone who had to go forward in the ship had to pass in the narrow passage by the cabinet. Thus, Watson would ensure a longer area of control over any arrival and at the same time get a long enough notice time to avoid being detected.

He brought the other three and immediately started loading the equipment onto the electric transport wheels that were taken in the truck. Within a couple of hours, most of them were unloaded on board the A1. The big control panels were built that way. Corbin cursed in a low voice as he pushed past to the required guard up in the attack center. However, he did not comment on the location.

Watson breathed out when he later met Phil Young in the galley. They just exchanged a short greeting and Young gave him a sugar cube at the coffee machine with one question to Watson, asking - "Do you want one"?

Back at the ballast controls, Watson read on the paper sheet that came with it:

"s.y. Thursday 12-16".

Young would obviously have a guard at the attack center next Thursday. This meant that photography would take place no later than that. The assembly would in any case be completed during Thursday and the A1 would probably leave Norway the same evening.

Watson concluded that he had to make use of Tonkin's pharmacy contact and disseminate the schedule for Fenella and Lenktov as soon as possible. Gerber was highly pleased with the course of the day and had no trouble laughing and waving to the guards at the exit gate. - "Nauseating types", Watson thought to himself.

Before leaving the hotel on their way to the base the next morning, Watson had already visited Lippke at the pharmacy and apparently delivered a prescription. Lippke had received all the necessary information about the progress in code on the "prescription" from Watson and forwarded it to Fenella who arrived at Rosenkranz Hotel from Stavanger the following day, Wednesday, November 8th. Tonkin was informed the same evening. Fenella at the same time confirmed that Watson and Gerber stayed at the hotel Neptune on the other side of the city just next to Hordaheimen Hotel, which she knew from before.

On the way into the base, Watson and Gerber passed the bus with the German navy boys, students from the hotel. Gerber had heard that the students would have a tour of the A1 during the day.

- "Good enough", answered Watson. - "Then we'll probably get it over and test how much time we have on Thursday, with that flock of people around!"

Reykjavik, Iceland, November 1970

At the same time, in Iceland in the Atlantic Ocean, 1000 km west of the action going on at Haakonsvern in Norway, a decisive struggle took place over time. Military intelligence was working full force to obtain possible new information for the CIA. The Icelanders felt they had a special responsibility in the case as they had hosted the A1. Already the same Wednesday as the message came from Conahan and the CIA, they had arrested Brit Jonsdottir. The cooperation between the two countries' intelligence services was excellent, primarily because the Americans had been responsible for the defense of the country that became a member of NATO after World War II. Together with a CIA man who had flown into Keflavik with B52 bombers via the American base at Thule in Greenland, they had for two days now tried to figure out what role she could have in any conspiracy that could have been implemented by the Russians or other communist countries. She denied knowing anything like that or having a relationship with the Young family other than that she previously lived with them for one year while on exchange. She claimed that she had never met Phil.

The intelligence officer, who had routinely implemented various control measures, had, among other things, also been confirmed by a photo lab in Reykjavik on Thursday that they had some pre-developed film for US Navy officers to be sent to Flensburg in Germany.

With the help of the criminal chief and a prosecutor, he was granted permission to review the pictures before they were forwarded.

The CIA had also provided the photo archive of the A1 crew. It turned out that most of the photos from the laboratory were of bathing in the Blue Lagoon and from Geysir during its eruptions. On Friday night , the intelligence service had found more pictures of Brit and Phil in the water, sitting and talking together. At a search at her home, a picture of Phil and Kelly was found from 1969 sitting in a restaurant, probably Spartacus in New York.

Taken in by the lies and presented with such convincing facts, Brit Jonsdottir failed to resist the pressure anymore and told them what she knew. She told them how she had become familiar with the environment around Kelly and that she had taken on the mission by being a messenger to her brother.

The intelligence agents realized quite quickly that she could not be particularly well informed or had any idea of the operation in which she participated. But the interrogations would still last for a long time and maybe lead to new tracks in this or other things.

In the evening a telex was sent to Conahan as confirmed by Jonsdottir's contact with Phil Young under the A1, the country's landing in Reykjavik. Late Thursday evening st before midnight, American time, Conahan received the message from Iceland at the ame time as the response to Young's questioning was received from the Atlantic ommand. The A1 was in open sea and without direct contact. In Norway the time was :00 a.m. Friday morning, and the A1 had left port eight hours earlier. Conahan nsidered the little finger and cursed in a low voice. Tonkin had the luck on his side gain.

otopsy

atson had a dry throat and was all sweaty as he sat next to Gerber on his way to the ase early on Thursday morning. The weather was beautiful and displayed the urroundings at its best, but that did not ease things for Watson.

The guards at the port spent more time than usual on the control and that did not ake things better either. - "Are you with the nuclear group?" the guard asked them in oor English. Gerber shook his head to show he did not understand and Watson bent orward and nodded, - "Yes, the technical team." The guard threw a final glance at the apers and waved his hand to sign that they could go on.

"What the hell is this?" Watson looked worriedly at Gerber. - "Either they have smelled omething or something else is going on! The control has been sharpened".

"If we notice anything else, we go full speed ahead." Watson carefully studied the urroundings to see if anything was different. As soon as they went around the building lose to the A1, they saw that all four guards armed with guns stood up, two on each side f the walkway. Until now there had only been one guard covering the entrance.

They were already so close to the boat that it would not be possible to return nnoticed. - "Okay, let's act normal. If they had been looking for us, they would not have tood there!" Watson jammed his elbow into Gerber's side to get him out of the car. ach with his equipment under his arm, they entered the walkway to the A1.

"Morning" They said to the guards.

"Papers please." One of the guards reached for his hand while the other three followed eir movements.

"Sorry, but we have a lot of visitors today and need to sharpen the check. But you now", the guard smiled and looked up from the papers. "We always have a large umber of researchers from the Kjeller-atom institute every time the atomic-team calls." e returned the passports and let them through.

"Have a nice day, sir", he nodded, smiling at Watson.

Watson was both happy and uneasy at the same time. It would not be easy to get ne job done with a lot of NATO people on board. But at the same time it would defuse ne activities so that they could more easily operate since everyone was busy oncentrating on the visitors.

Phil Young joined them in the hallway with a sign around his neck indicating that e was the officer in command. - "Good morning boys, ready for today's conquest?" He ung sharply toward Watson and nodded politely to Gerber. Watson was momentarily onfused by Phil's nonchalant appearance, wondering if the guy was sentient and aware f the risk he was facing, but he quickly turned away from it.

They quickly agreed to go a little further down the hallway from the control room towards the cabin of the captain so that they would not be too disturbed by all the visitors.

Watson was relatively familiar with the Norwegian nuclear energy conditions Tonkin had given him a thorough review as part of the briefing on Bergen and the Håkon Conservation Base. The main objective of Lippke's intelligence in the region was to keep track of activities at the base, primarily related to marine nuclear power.

The only nuclear reactor in Norway was in Halden and set up by the Energy Technique Institute in 1958. The plan was to build nuclear power plants in Norway and to develop nuclear reactors for the propulsion of ships. Norway played an important role during the war and in the years after war as a manufacturer of heavy water for use in nuclear power and bomb manufacturing in many countries. Initially, the justification for supporting the project was precisely to help Norwegian industry to produce nuclear reactors such as propulsion machinery in merchant ships. Eventually, the purpose was changed to keep track of international nuclear technology development in general.

One of IFE-Kjeller's most important operating areas so far was the operation of the spent nuclear fuel reprocessing plants. Calls from NATO nuclear submarines to the base in Bergen eventually became a lucrative business for the research institute. The need to get rid of spent radioactive fuel was intrusive and Kjeller's offer of radio activation was highly appreciated. Therefore, for the KGB's people in Norway, it was relatively easy to register calls for nuclear submarines. With an almost 99% safety record, they could span the Kjeller researchers' trips to Western Norway and northern Norway and locate nuclear submarines. It was almost too easy.

Watson shook the thoughts from his mind and took his bag that had been hanging from the door. - "Let's find the issues and get started. The repair should be completed today." He nodded to Young.
- "We need to make sure that it's a bit too tight for someone to pass in the hallway where we work", he continued, - "And you must always move between the cabin and the walkway to get a full overview of traffic on board and outside."
- "The captain is far away. The base manager and a representative from Kjeller invited us on a ferry trip by rail over Flom to Sognefjord and by boat back to Bergen late tonight. We will not be surprised by him", replied Phil.
- "Great, that means we probably have more options. That's all right." Watson nodded pleased. He immediately had Gerber start installing the panels that stood at the front of the entrance, and he himself began to install others a little further. The big back with the photo equipment stood along the wall, close to him, towards the captain's cabin.
- "I think you simply have to take the chance to unlock the cabin", Watson said to Phil.
- "No one will check it now when the captain is awake. This allows you to quickly enter."

Phil nodded and walked quickly to the door and twisted the key in the lock. He put the key in his pocket and squeezed past Watson back into the hallway. Soon they heard voices and Watson caught a glimpse of Phil at the very end of the hall, with a hand to his cap. Lieutenant Corbin suddenly appeared in the entrance in front of a row of six or seven visitors. He greeted Phil and presented the guests. - "This is a group of atomic researchers from Norway and Germany. I am giving them a short round in the engine section." He turned his head back and nodded in the direction of the operating center.

Watson relaxed as soon as he heard what Corbin said. It did not matter if the people went to the reactor. On the contrary, they would be safer knowing where they were and could work in peace and quiet. He suddenly realized that he was pushed up to the cabin door and that the sweat ran down his back. He cursed himself and went back towards the panels.

After Corbin and his group had left the ship again, Phil returned to the hallway. The time had elapsed at 11:30 and it was lunchtime at the base. All visitors were in or on their way to the canteen with their respective guides.

- "Okay, lets get started now", said Phil as he had crossed Gerber and was getting near Watson.

- "Gerber coughs twice if anyone arrives, while ensuring nobody is able to pass. He coughs once when it is clear", Watson replied. He looked over to Gerber who coughed to make a sign.

- "Start!" Watson said to Phil. Phil bent down over the bag with the oscilloscope and twisted the container with the lens and the camera. He looked to both sides to make sure everything was clear and nodded to Watson as he pushed the door open and went back into the cabin. Watson saw him disappear and the door closed behind him.

He stood right in front of the door and watched the hallway and entrance hall. They had agreed on warning signs. One knock on the door meant everything was ready. Two meant that Phil had to wait and three, that the situation was hopeless and that they would probably be revealed. In that case, it was up to the individual to improvise or, at worst, chew holes in the cyanide capsule Watson had provided everyone with.

Gerber was deep in though and had no intention of going that far. Phil worked frantically. He lifted off the sheets on the bunk and searched with his hands for the folder containing the protocols. The first thing he discovered was the captain's personal gun that lay by the headboard. The folder was a mass production and closed with a simple lock that Phil had already obtained by a key Tonkin had given him, having contacted the manufacturer and put a copy in the camera container.

The lock was opened. He opened the folder and put it close to the small desk with the light bulb. The camera and the film were designed precisely to be able to operate with a lamp and without flash. He tried to pick out the right sides and recognized the maps with the formation and the basic strategic fleet positions. He knew that each nuclear submarine had its fixed launch position by mobilization. The following pages clearly contained a complete attack and operation description for the entire fleet. By supporting the camera against one of the books on the shelf ("The Deepest Reason" by Graham Greene), he got photos of 19 pages. The air intake on the wall was so quiet that he did not hear any sounds from the outside. Unknowingly, he stated that this was significantly more serious than he had previously done for the Russians and probably qualified for the death penalty. At the same time, he realized that the sweat dropped from his nose and spread beyond the side of the folder and pulled a sheet of the bed over his forehead to dry it. He suddenly felt cold and scared. However, with his background from submarine training to cope with more difficult situations, he quickly gained self-control and locked the folder before pushing it back into place under the bed behind the gun. The bed linen was laid out as it had been before and he put the book back in the shelf, but upside down. He couldn't do anything else, besides wait for Watson.

Watson's nerves were tense like bowstrings. During the three to four minutes, another group of visitors had boarded. Lieutenant Corbin returned from the operating center and brought two especially interested people to which he would show the operation and command place. He passed Gerber, who coughed and said, - "Sorry", to

Watson, "can we get past you?" Watson smiled and nodded, - "Of course, it's a bit cramped, but otherwise you should be able to go." He hoped the door would not open.

Corbin stayed for about five minutes before returning and passed Watson on his way out.

- "Have you seen Young anywhere?" he asked while passing.

- "He is getting some food, I think", Watson replied and nodded. Corbin quickly forgot the subject when he met with the visitors, as they were about to leave the boat.

Watson had thought Corbin could see how nervous he was. Almost quivering. He was brought back to reality by Gerber's coughing sound further down the hallway.

- "Clear track!" He hit Phil's door that almost opened and moved quickly out.

He put the camera down in the bag with Watson and concealed the entrance with his back while locking the door. Smiling, he passed Watson with his thumb on his right hand lifted and said, - "Have a nice day gentlemen" and greeted them before putting the key into Watson's bag and walking down the hallway.

Watson shook his head. - "The guy is hell, and I'm crazy. A cold fish" he thought and bent down to push the camera container back into place.

- "Done! Done! Incredible"! Happiness burst through his head.

Gerber was almost ready for the retrofitting and their work on board was over in about two hours. They assembled tools and equipment and got help from one of the guards to carry everything back to the car. Just before departure, Corbin and Phil were both in place again, and Watson thanked them for the help and asked them to greet the captain when he returned. Both of them cheered as they left the ship and wished them a good trip home. Outside the base and clear of the checkout Watson sat down in the seat and shouted loudly and joyfully!

On their way back to the hotel, they agreed to have minimum contact for the next two days. Gerber was going to take the car with the equipment to Kristiansand on Saturday morning and then over to Hirtshals by ferry on Sunday night.

Watson was to stay in Bergen until Monday November 23, to meet Fenella and then travel by flight from Flesland airport. As agreed with Tonkin, Watson changed the film the same evening with the one he had bought earlier. Gerber was not aware of this. However, he was advised to carefully take care of the tool and the camera along the way, keeping the bag locked until he was contacted in Flensburg. Watson was fully aware that both he and Gerber could be in the spotlight if something had leaked to the CIA. The risk was too big for some of them to bring the film out.

The same was true of Tonkin's other fixed network. Fenella, on the other hand, was unknown and could not be linked with the operation in the same way. He decided to keep calm in the hotel for the next few days and had some contact with some of the Germans who were in training at Haakonsvern to obtain information if possible.

At breakfast on Saturday morning he heard that the big American nuclear submarine had left the base on Friday night. He put his hand into his pocket and felt the little key he had laid there the night before. It was for the cabin that belonged to the captain of the world's most advanced submarine.

On Friday morning on the way past the mobile oil drilling vessels in the Ekkofisk area of the North Sea, Commander Janson went down to the cabin to pick up the operating instructions. He found what he needed from under the bed sheet and seized the door handle to close it but stopped abruptly. He turned to the little bookshelf and pulled out "Greene" with his index finger. To his surprise the book was in an upright position and he knew he hadn't left it that way. He pushed the book into place right away. - "Well I may have", he thought with a shrug before he left the room

Bergen - New York, November 20, 1970

Later that day when the A1 left Bergen city, Tromboli drove south towards the city, and landed on one of the ferries in Nordhordaland. The clock already showed 17:00 in the afternoon. Yet they had an hour left before they were in the hotel, at least he and Zana. Lenktov was likely to be in the car.

He had called hotels in Loen from Aleksandra and booked two single rooms at Scandia Hotel, close to the Bergen Railway Station.
- "I lived there two years ago so that should be useful", he said to Lenktov and Zana.
- "As far as I remember, they also have a decent parking space close by", he nodded to Lenktov.

Lenktov, who knew the hotel from Fenella's itinerary, just smiled back and pulled his shoulders back. - "It will be fine. Real Russian bears do not go to sleep in winter, you know. "Never sleep" as Khrushchev said!"

Zana, who had been unsure if something would be changed with regard to the two single rooms, laughed out loud in a liberating fashion,
- "We shall leave the whiskey in the car again. Bears do like honey also don't they?" They kept talking and joking with each other until they reached the hotel. Lenktov noticed a tense and nervous undertone behind Zana's apparently easy and sociable talk. Tromboli would in any case pay close attention to what she was doing at the hotel. Lenktov was still unsure whether anything was wrong with Zana's behavior. He had seen her purchase the film in Trondheim, but it could be innocent and for her own purpose. But he had to take precautions.

The car got an excellent location in its own garage in a building next to the hotel and Lenktov could even lock and close or possibly leave the car and take shorter city tours without anyone wondering if he went out or into the garage.

The need to call Conahan was eventually so intrusive to Zana that Tromboli asked if she had become ill after driving. She showed her fatigue and managed to let him go to his room just before 11:00 p.m despite the risk, she quickly decided to call Conahan. She imagined that he had to be pretty annoyed after waiting almost a day for her to call.

She contacted the hotel front desk and was told that she would not be charged if the hotel called a phone number and received confirmation to call back.

Conahan was about to leave the office when he received a message to call the hotel in Norway. He dialed the number and immediately recognized Zana's voice. She spoke quietly and fast and asked him to take notes.
- "On Monday, the Russians will hand over a film of images of NATO's defense strategies and naval strategic placements in the North Atlantic and Northern Europe, thereby causing significant damage. Tonkin is responsible for the operation that is the top priority in the Kremlin and is called Isotopsy. I can prevent this by switching the film, but want a deal with you to do it. I want one million dollars and a residence permit in the United States. In addition, you have to get me a cabin on the Norwegian Hurtigruten from Trondheim on Tuesday or on a helicopter to the boat earlier. I also want a new identity."

She stopped for a moment and then continued, - "It will not help if you track me down or contact Norwegian intelligence. If so, I will not get the film. Hardly anyone else will either".

Conahan grunted unhappily at the other end. He understood the seriousness of the matter. He knew Zana and he knew Tonkin. He quickly recounted that this was an ultimatum and that he did not want time to confer with the senior staff or risk reconnecting with Zana.

- "O.K. I guarantee you get your agreement, provided that the film is correct. We will probably pick you up on the boat. You'll have to wait and see".

- "Before I board the boat, I will send the film to a hotel in Oslo by post in a parcel with my own name." said Zana.

- "You will be given the name as soon as we are on our way to the United States".

- "It's okay, we only get the embassy to pick it up. Good luck!" Conahan laid down the receiver and breathed out.

- "Finally, an opening! This will go well for me!" He contacted the secretary at the Defense department and agreed to meet with the secretary the next morning at 09:00. He also managed to arrange an immediate meeting with the FBI in New York and the US representative for Interpol.

Everyone was duly informed about the situation except for the name, place and time of the agreement with Zana. The connections were now apparent with the A1's call in Flensburg, the strange movements of the Russians in Rome and London and not least the Papadakis murder to hide the track back to the Young family.

- "We do not know what documents the Russians can get. We also do not know if Phil Young on board the A1 can give us more information. He is also not available for questioning. But we've been following the operation for a long time, and it's because Tonkin is leading it all, there's no doubt that NATO and the United States will come in a particularly critical situation if we're unable to put an end to it. Certain types of information from the A1 are of the highest security rating and of importance to the defense balance. If we are wrong here, the Russians will push us on all fronts, both in Vietnam, the Middle East and in Europe. The Russian approach to China is disturbing and a serious threat that can be reinforced by a new situation in the northern regions".

Conahan paused for a while and then continued, - "I think unfortunately we have to trust that Zana is doing her part. In any case, we cannot risk intervening too early. I certainly do not want anyone to destroy the operation in Norway now!" Conahan nodded strictly to the man from Interpol.

- "We can do a search in cooperation with Norwegian POT and our own embassy. They will have to arrange the retrieval of Zana and the film. That's going to go well. The really big issue we have here is what Tonkin chooses to do and where he is at the moment. We know from our people in Norway that one of Russia's KGB people at the embassy in Oslo, Lenktov, was in Trondheim just a week ago, without reporting his travels according to protocol. However, he returned the same evening. There are indications that Zana Jankaan came to Bergen from Trondheim, not least because she sent the telegram from Kristiansund. There is most likely a connection there".

They continued the talks and discussion for over an hour before concluding that Conahan had full support in running the operation as he wished. All parties supported his decision to fulfill Zana's demands, which was necessary before the meeting with the efense secretary. Conahan intentionally told them that the hotel in Bergen was already nder surveillance.

enktov moved softly on the stained carpet in the hallway outside the door to Zana's oom, as soon as he heard her pick up the phone receiver. The old hotel had poor solation, almost like the old grass barns in Tomsk! Lenktov heard most of Zana's onversation with Conahan. He noticed that she said she would post the film before she oarded the Hurtigruten. In other words, it meant that the Americans would only have o wait in uncertainty to discover what she would send or indeed whether they would get nything at all. Lenktov decided to try to reach Tonkin on the phone to notify him of ecent events.

enella was relieved her stay in Stavanger was over. She paid the hotel bill and got the elp of the taxi driver to carry her suitcases out to the taxi. After buying a ticket to ergen at the reception on the pier, she boarded and sat down in the comfortable cabin f the hydrofoil boat with the powerful Viking name Vingtor that would bring her to the nal stage of Operation Isotopsy.

She looked forward to the beautiful trip along the coast after waiting in tavanger. But even more she looked forward to meeting Lenktov again. However, she ad to be extremely careful in Bergen. NATO undoubtedly had its people placed in nportant places. Tonkin had informed her that one of his people would stay at osenkranz and Neptun hotels as an additional precaution if something went wrong. He anted his room to be on the 4th floor. They were not to show that they knew each other, ither in the restaurant or elsewhere.

Ever since they left each other in Paris, Fenella had been looking forward to 1eeting Nika again. She had even called and confirmed at one of the high-mountain otels between Bergen and Oslo and was assured that there were available double ooms.

The seriousness of the mission was almost different, and she had to resort to 1inking of her parents to come back to reality. She closed her eyes while the boat lifted er like a steep stallion to the humming of the engines that set off for Bergen.

From the speedboat terminal in Bergen she quickly got a taxi to the hotel osenkranz. After taking a look at the room she asked if she could switch to a different oom without a balcony on the 4th floor. Tonkin had been fully aware of these points. here was to be minimal predictability and maximum security. She reserved the room or one night.

During the evening she met with Tonkin's man who came knocking on her door. 1e brought the piece of paper from Lippke with the messages from Watson, including a onfirmed meeting time and place. After a brief conversation, he left the room and later onveyed to Tonkin that Fenella was in place according to the plan.

The next day she moved to the hotel Hordaheimen, near the hotel Neptun and ear Watson. The room was on the 4th floor and only had a tiny little window, in line rith Tonkin's instructions.

Tonkin's co-worker also checked in to hotel Neptun that day. Neither he nor Vatson knew each other's identity or mission. Lenktov was on his way to Bergen.

The USS A1 left Bergen late that evening.

New York – Copenhagen, November 1970

Conahan quickly decided to travel to Europe. He slept most of the trip through Iceland to Denmark. Early on Sunday morning he was driving along Old Køge Landevei on the way from Kastrup Airport to a meeting at the embassy in Copenhagen.

Two German intelligence officers in Bonn and Berlin, the Swedish and Norwegian navy attorneys, the head of Interpol in Paris, NATO's Secretary-General and two NATO intelligence personnel attended the meeting.

Conahan briefed them on the case and presented the scenario that could develop into a problem.

What will happen if Zana Jankaan does not want to or cannot fulfill the agreement? What do we do then? And how will they try to bring out the film?, were some of the questions they discussed possible answers to.

We do not know exactly what the film contains, other than that in addition to the positions of nuclear-submarines, it is about NATO's strategic defense plans and defense positions in northern Europe. We also know that Tonkin is the leader of the operation.

Most nodded to the last. Intelligence in all NATO countries knew of the "Tonkin Organization". One of the NATO representatives spoke,
- "There are many possibilities. There are air bases, navy bases, rocket bases or even something else. However, we need to take this seriously. Even though we change the strategy, it will cost us enormously, and at the same time, the Russians will see how we plan and think. That will be a disaster! Knowing that Tonkin is behind this, should tell us the level of seriousness. We cannot take this matter easy." The Norwegian attendant nodded.
- "We have reason to believe that Tonkin came to Trondheim via Sweden and that he will send the film out that way and. But it could also go south to Denmark - Germany or north to Finland and from there to Russia. We will ensure significantly increased border control. Particularly on the ferries", He looked at his Swedish colleague and asked him to confirm that they would also increase their border control.
- "Clearly", the Swede answered. "We have also received confirmation from the defense minister that we can expand the controls in the ports, especially in the areas around Stockholm", he added.

Everyone in attendance listened carefully to the Swedish statements, not least with the latest reports of Russian submarines' activities, like the fjords outside of Stockholm, in mind.

Conahan broke the silence and spoke again. - "Good, but I'm sure we need to get a search team to Bergen immediately, both at the Haakonsvern base and strategic places around the city." I will arrange this with our people and POT in Norway and of course he nodded to the Interpol boss and the two intelligence men from NATO.
- "If we haven't resolved this by Monday – we will set up new guidelines for strategic and tactical crews throughout Northern Europe and major parts of the Atlantic Ocean on Tuesday."
- "An informal ministerial meeting has already taken place, which has provided us with the mandate to act immediately if need be," stated the Secretary General.
- "And according to our American colleagues, it will be up to you to inform us on time, he confirmed with his eyes on Conahan.

"Thank you", Conahan smiled happily back, - "we have our little happy moments here n life! But, you will always be continuously oriented on direct lines, and will be as pdated as me. It will hardly be a difficult decision to take for anyone. Besides, we may ave some luck for once!"

He thanked everyone for attending the meeting and asked the four investigators o stay behind to discuss further information together with POT Norway and Interpol.

On Sunday night, NATO's two investigators from the meeting were picked up by POT at the Bergen airport and driven to Hotel Neptun and Scandia in Bergen. After a hort briefing later in the evening, both returned to their hotels and to bed.

For safety reasons, Conahan had not yet informed them that Zana was staying at he Scandia Hotel. One of them would board the northbound Hurtigrute, the following lay, and accompany passengers with the necessary signal to Zana and instructions on ow to deal with her if she should appear there. The other agent wanted to go to the ase and see if he could find out how the film had been released.

But Conahan was not calm at all. The tingling feeling in the shoulder blades was tronger than ever. What worried him most was that, without her knowledge, Tonkin ould use Zana as a diversion. In that case he would probably take the film through the ncorporated courier channels across the border with Russia from Northern Norway.

t was therefore a simple decision for Conahan to let the CIA and counter-espionage ctivate the network and initiate the border guard procedures drawn up between Norway and the United States for the border along Russia in crisis situations. He even prepared to go to Bergen the following morning.

Keflavik, Iceland, November 23

Phil Young had been questioned at the base since early in the morning. He was lready confronted with the fact that Brit had revealed and told all about the transfer nd relationship with Kelly and Phil. He did not even know what had happened to Kelly nd completely broke down when he was told that she had been imprisoned and held in ustody by the CIA and charged with treason. With the view of a death sentence hanging ver him, he felt compelled to co-operate.

Conahan, who had arrived in Bergen early in the afternoon, received a call in the oom he had just checked in to hotel Norge. It was the head of mission at the base in Keflavik who called to brief him.

In order not to interfere with the outcome of the deal with Zana, he contacted the nterpol boss who attended the meeting in Copenhagen and sent out inquiries for Gerber and Watson from there, according to Phil Young's descriptions. At the same ime, one of the two German intelligence officers who had come to Bergen was informed o that the workshop in Flensburg could be contacted and the two arrested.

Conahan personally called the Secretary-General of NATO and informed him bout what information was likely to have been stolen from the A1. He gave a short priefing on the possibilities of preventing the information from reaching the Russians nd a calculation of how great the chances were of success. He freed the Secretary-General to take the necessary precautions and measures, but asked for a three-day leadline to solve the problem.

The Secretary-General thought about it for a moment and then agreed to Conahan's suggestions.

- "You have two days. If we do not find the film by then, we will change the entire strategic and tactical defense structure in NATO, and in the Pacific, and Northern regions, and restructure all Atlantic sea and land positions".

Conahan breathed out, but the drama of the statement sent a cloud of confused questions around his head. He tried to retain himself and answered calmly, - "All right, sir, we may be able to do it. I expect to be assisted by your two representatives here if you will arrange to brief them. Thank you again sir." He hung up the phone.

- "Damn! Most often, they are so reluctant to make a decision that the Russians must cry with laughter." Conahan hit his hands together with a bang. Soon after, the undercover officers came from Zana's hotel and went up to the room after calling from the front desk. He could tell that she was no longer in the hotel, but it had not been possible to find out how or where she had gone. He had followed the order not to follow her so close that she became suspicious. The situation vexed Conahan, but it would be difficult to blame the agent.

They were thereby referred to keep the Hurtigrute passengers under supervision. A review of the preliminary passenger list told him nothing. The three other investigators from the NATO meeting and two of his own from Oslo were deployed on and in the area around the Hurtigrute harbor.

The first day after leaving Norway, Gerber's thoughts had only revolved around how he could utilize the film he had found in the toolbox, for his own benefit. No one had contacted him in Flensburg and he began to think that something went wrong with Watson and that the Russians might not know that it was he himself who had the film. After weighing his options for a long time, he decided to contact the Americans and sell the film to them. He called the embassy in Berlin and told them who he was and that he had valuable intelligence material stolen from the Russians. The Ambassador who received the call took it seriously and informed the German Ministry of Foreign Affairs and the CIA. He also agreed to meet Gerber in Hamburg.

The Russian's man in the Brandt administration quickly picked up the information from the Americans to the Foreign Ministry and immediately conveyed the information to Tonkin's people in northern Germany.

The CIA was unable to link the information to the case in Norway right away and only after Conahan, sent out the information about Gerber and Watson, after hearing about Phil Young, the connection was clear.

As he travelled south to Hamburg, Gerber was unaware of being wanted by the German police. He drove early and remained willingly away from the highway to avoid being delayed by accidents or other things.

A black Mercedes passed him just before a curve. The car had CC plates and Gerber, who had the meeting in mind, followed the car with extra attention. In a moment, he realized that it had been sent to escort him to the embassy and smiled happily. The car reduced speed in the middle of the curve and suddenly the front of his own car was pushed out of the way by a big pick-up road service truck with a crane, which was positioned near the rear of the car. He almost stood on the brake and almost stopped the car before it hit a tree and he hit his head against the wheel.

As Gerber did not appear at the meeting with the embassy receptionist who was now aware of the request from the CIA, the man again contacted the Ministry of Foreign

Affairs. In a matter of hours they were familiar with the surprising accident and had the police search the car.

Conahan was informed later in the evening in Bergen in Norway. It was assumed that some of the equipment that was gone could have been used for "hidden" photo shoots. No film was found. Gerber was alive but severely injured and unconscious.

- "Fooled again!" Conahan was clearly furious. - "Someone must have been silenced". He informed the German intelligence man who was in the hotel,

- "Why the hell has it become like this, because of the reason you showed thirty years ago? It's like a leaking strainer in your foreign ministry!"

- "But sir!", answered the German eagerly and a little provoked. - "We have already announced a review of the administration. This case clearly indicates that the leak came from there".

- "Actually, I do not think this episode plays any part whatsoever", Conahan answered. "Gerber traveled from Bergen long before Zana was to retrieve the film. He didn't have anything and at best he is fooled to deluded. But you must find the mole, that is for sure!"

- "I'm more worried if we hear something from your lady right now", said the German. Conahan threw a sharp look at him to see if the guy was being flippant. But no, they had a problem, clearly. For safety he gave his own people the message to call Zana and Watson through the agency network.

- "Continue to put pressure on your people in Germany so we might come to grips with the American who was with Gerber. You may have a little luck with it at least". Conahan said the last sentence too low to be understood by the German. He felt helpless and his frustration was not to hide.

Chapter 9

ISDALEN VALLEY, November 23

Fenella woke up at six o'clock as the phone on the nightstand rang loudly. She sat up in her bed, picked up the receiver and said "Good morning". Nika Lenktov enjoyed hearing her voice again. - "Hello Fenella, Long time, no see! It's just me". Fenella woke up and imagined the heat from Lenktov's body. - "Finally!" Fenella thought, "I've been waiting for you", she replied. - "Long. Way too long!" She turned over on her back, placed the phone receiver on her shoulder and stared unconcerned into the ceiling as she pictured the image of Lenktov's smiling face.

- "You understand the agreement with Watson?" he said. - "Yes", Fenella replied and was quickly back in reality. - "Then we meet as agreed at 12:00 o'clock at the meeting place. Zana and I will arrive as a "jogging couple".

First take a taxi to the railway storage and a then another taxi from there. Wear your clothes. And take out the rest of the tour equipment from the suitcases and bring it with you. If we had to travel straight ahead for some reason or leave our suitcases, at least we need to have it with us".

- "Have you heard anything new from T about Tr or C"? Fenella had to ask. Both knew that it was Tonkin's message from Trondheim about Tromboli and if the CIA was on track after them.

- "Both yes and no", Lenktov answered diplomatically. "But we're uncertain and it's important that you go through your suitcases and equipment once more and make sure all marks and labels are removed. If necessary, take what you cannot remove and burn it up in the valley. There is a lot at stake and if something goes wrong, it should not be possible to trace you from the suitcases whether we take them with us or not!"

- "I'll go through them again, but everything should be alright already", said Fenella.

- "Good luck", said Lenktov before they both hung up.

Fenella lay back in bed for a moment and thought of Lenktov before getting up and to the shower across the hallway. As usual, she carefully locked the door and nodded to the maid who was making her rounds with bed linen and towels.

At twenty past nine, she walked out of the reception area, but kept the room key with her. She continued to the right, walked up the narrow Holtegårdsmuget and turned to the left along the narrow Strandgaten before she apparently and accidentally stood at one of the shop windows in Sundtgården and looked sideways into the shop against the bank desk of Bergen's privat bank which was close to the entrance. With her right eye, she noticed that Watson came walking towards her on the street from the opposite direction. She stood as if she were studying the store window, while he, without looking at her, turned right into the main entrance. Fenella saw through the window that he continued past the bank into the store and toward Herreekvipering Branch. She had a burning desire to meet his eyes and was about to follow them, when she suddenly noticed a person who was browsing through a booklet in the bank while looking over at Watson. Fenella felt her heart rate increase and instead went straight to the bank desk and exchanged some German marks for Norwegian kronas. The man did not seem to notice her. She continued into the store past Watson and bought a scarf that she put in a plastic bag and went to the leisure clothes department where she stood between two acks watching prices and sizes of windbreakers. She put the plastic bag down on the oor next to her.

Watson remained in the store and as he passed Fenella he let a small package slip nnoticed into the bag on the floor. He continued to look at clothes and walked out of 1e shop shortly after. She noticed that the other man left the store soon after. With her ag in her left hand she walked out and back to the hotel. Although she was very uneasy, he realized that it was a coincidence that the man looked at Watson and that she was 1ore tense than usual.

Glad to have Norwegian money, she went straight to the small reception desk at 1e hotel and asked to pay for the room. She paid in cash and returned the copy of the ill, in the name of Elisabeth Leenhouwfr.

"Goodbye Mrs. Lenhåfer", (In German) said the receptionist with a smile. Back in 00m 407, Fenella immediately locked the door and fetched a calming pill, which she wallowed with a glass of water. She picked up the package from Watson, opened it, and und that the container with the film roll was in place. The thought of the content made er breathe quickly. She shoved the roll down into the side pocket of the little bag ogether with the equipment Lenktov had asked her to bring. She made sure that there as no trace left of her before leaving the room. She even took the Norwegian ewspaper Dagbladet, she had bought on Saturday after seeing the picture of the priest om the Montessori in Rome on the frontpage.

The two suitcases were not too heavy so she brought them down to the front desk y herself, where she dropped them just outside the doorway. She came out the door nd saw a free taxi and waived. The driver noticed her waiving, continued a bit, turned nd drove up to the front of the entrance.

At a quarter past ten on Monday morning, Fenella, with the name Elisabeth eenhouwfr, left Hordaheimen as planned. With the man from the bank fresh in her 1emory, she looked around in all directions as the taxi drove away from the hotel.

That same morning Lenktov was ready in the car outside the Scandia Hotel and /aited for Zana. He had changed to light exercise clothes and sneakers and during the ight he had gotten the Luger pistol from under the car. He took no chances and had the un in a holster under his right arm. Just as Tonkin had taught him, he had suspended 1e light metal container with naphtha that was useful both as an anesthetic and a fire gent. He kept that under his left arm.

Zana had been sitting together with Tromboli at breakfast and rehearsed the plan nd agreed to a meeting place and time. She complained of headaches despite having aking tablets and was visibly nervous. Tromboli assumed that it was a natural reaction ue to the responsibility of transporting the film. He clasped her on her shoulder and aid in Italian, - "Non ti preoccupare", meaning don't worry.

She was already dressed for the ride and the meeting with a small purse, wool weater, sports pants and sneakers. She took the bag with her other belongings to romboli's room at eleven o'clock in the morning. He arranged payment at the hotel and 1en took Zana's luggage to bring to the passenger ship "Hurtigruten".

Lenktov helped her get the little suitcase into the car and noticed that she seemed ss self-confident than she used to be. Usually Zana was full of sarcasm and ambiguous okes.

"And you're ready for a real jogging trip", he smiled irritatingly to her as he sat own behind the steering-wheel of "Giovanni Tromboli" with his driver's license under his own photo. He did not want to give Zana the impression that he was tense or that there was something other unusual going on.

At the side entrance of the railway station, Fenella paid for the taxi and went into the storage area with the two suitcases. With the leather hat in her hand and the little tour-bag dangling over her left shoulder, she continued straight back to the taxiline on the eastern side and got a new car to drive her to Isdalen valley.

The taxi stopped at the buildings just in front of the entrance to the valley. A cold wind allowed her to pull the veil and pull the big scarf around her face as soon as she got out of the car. The weather was cloudy and misty, but without rain. She quickly walked up the steep hill at the dam at the end of the valley, and continued deliberately along the way inwards. Occasionally she stopped and looked back. The large mountain on the right side could be seen in the water below her. She passed some workmen with a service car, some joggers and a couple of hikers whom she watched carefully without further notice. She stopped for a moment on a bench in the curve near the quarry and caught a glimpse of the television mast on Ulrikken. The mountain appeared majestic in an opening in the cloud cover.

Upon her arrival at the path that Lippke had shown her, she went off from the road and up to the little clearance where she sat on a rock and opened the bag. Thanks to the rubber boots she had bought in Stavanger, her legs were dry after the trip in the slightly humid terrain.

She still had several of the passports intact, but only retained one with Zana's identity. She put them between some stones and poured gasoline from the small bottle over the first. As she stood bowed, she suddenly heard a branch crack and got a glimpse of a person in the area closer to the road. She grabbed the other passes and shoved them in her pocket, while fingering for the matchbox, took off her gloves to get a match, and quickly lit the petrol-covered passport.

Zana and Lenktov walked across the valley, Zana with the little bag on her back. She breathed heavily after having taken sedative pills, because she was so nervous just before they left the hotel. The low cloud cover in the valley meant that the visual view was slight and limited. The high mountains that encircled the deep sea could only be nested in the rocks that plunged into the water.

Zana thought about what would happen further along as she struggled to keep up with Lenktov. Just in case, she had previously put one of the two films in an envelope stamped and delivered to the hotel postal services. She had decided not to risk having the plans changed. The other was placed between the clothes at the bottom of the canvas.

She had decided to mislead as much as she could by sending a fake film in the mail but retaining the other in order to be able to change it and be safer to cope with Conahan until he brought her to safety away from Tromboli on Hurtigruten. She was glad she had not revealed to Conahan that Tromboli travelled with her.

They approached a small ridge in the middle of the valley, and Lenktov steered them towards a bench where they sat for a moment and rested. He was late to meet Fenella, but at the same time deeply concentrated on the situation with the CIA that Tonkin had informed him about.

There were very few people along the road this cold Monday morning in November and after they passed the bridge and proceeded towards the end of the lake hey saw no one else. Lenktov went off the path from the road and proceeded toward a lense plantation. At the same moment he saw a strong glow between the tree trunks.

Sitting in front of the little fire, Fenella saw, to her happiness, that it was Lenktov he had heard and seen a glimpse of just before. Her pulse rate fell significantly after she saw him when he came out of the forest with Zana just behind him.

"Nika! Zana! You found each other?" she asked without waiting for answers.

"No problem for an old young pioneer! In addition, you must have just burned something that we saw so clearly". He nodded towards the little fire that had not yet been burned down.

"Lots of unnecessary papers no one needs anymore", She smiled almost lovingly at Lenktov.

"Good to see you again", he said in a low voice.

"Hello, Fenella, you look as good as before!" Zana was breathless and she had sunglasses on her head over her hair. She had her hair in a little ponytail, just like Fenella.

The fire that Fenella had lit had already burned down and only a slight strip of smoke rose.

"Can we finish as soon as possible so I can leave?" Zana asked.

"Do you have the film Fenella"? - "Yes, everything has gone well so far", Fenella answered. - "But let's finish exchanging clothes and boots first so I'll be a proper jogger and you a presentable hiking lady!" Fenella pulled off the quilted jacket and gave it to Zana, together with the big scarf. Zana threw her the running shoes. She sat down on a stone and delivered one boot to Zana, who immediately began to pull it on.

"Wait!" Lenktov interrupted them and spoke suddenly and loudly with a sharp and different voice.

The change was so striking that Fenella immediately moved and put the other boot down between the rocks.

"What in..."she got so far when she discovered Lenktov with the Luger pistol pointing at them. Zana stared at him, scared and backed away.

"What the hell are you doing? Have you gone completely out of your mind? What do you think Tonkin will say?" She spoke frantically while constantly staring at the gun pointing at her. Lenktov continued to hold the gun directed at her while he bent down and took up the bag that he threw towards Fenella.

"Look in the bag and tell me what you find", he ordered her. Fenella turned the bag upside down and emptied the contents on the ground. Between Zana's clothes, some cosmetics and a box of pills, she picked up the film.

"What do we have here?" Lenktov directed his question to Zana.

"It's just an unexposed film that I'll use later. What else?" she responded with assumed credibility.

"Sorry Zana, but the game is over. We've been following you ever since you bought the film in Trondheim and we know you called the CIA to betray us. Tonkin knows every word you exchanged from the hotel with agent Conahan! We know you wanted to change the film and let the Americans get the original".

This time, Zana was stiffening and became noticeably paler. She looked completely exhausted. - "I'm not going to betray anyone. All I wanted was to trick the Americans. You must believe me." She looked, almost praying to Fenella.

- "How about Gerber and Watson, how about Kelly and us? How did you think we would escape the Americans after giving them information about the operation? And how in the hell would Tromboli survive that situation?" continued Lenktov. He thought of the cyanide caps they had made, in case something went wrong.

Zana looked very stressed and talked with a crying voice while staring at the gun.
- "You cannot do this to me!"
- "What agreement do you have?" Lenktov asked while lifting the gun with no restraint.
- "They do not know anything about Tromboli or you! I was going to board the boat and get picked up along the way or in Trondheim." The words poured like a waterfall out of Zana's mouth.
- "Fenella", she said, "this has nothing to do with you. I no longer manage Tonkin and his cases. The only way out for me is America!"

Fenella, who would never understand how someone could betray the communist ideas she had sacrificed so much for, thought for a moment of the newspaper article on her executed parents, and then looked at Zana with disgust and with a hateful expression. - "Traitor" she breathed between her teeth.

Lenktov lifted the gun and Zana took a step backward and the back of her knees buckled and she fell between the rocks. He moved the gun over to his left hand as he grabbed the pill-glass that lay close by, opened it and forced her to open her mouth while looking coldly into her eyes. - "Russia is able without the help of its enemies. Enemies of the Soviet Union!"

He forced her to swallow some of the pills. Zana stared paralyzed as Lenktov lightly lifted his right arm over her left shoulder and delivered a deadly stroke down against the collarbone and cervical vein on her right side. She moved under the violent power of the concentrated hit and her head fell forward as if on a dangling rag roll. The sunglasses loosened from the hair and crushed against a stone and the lifeless figure remained sitting on her knees in a kind of a hole between the large stones.

Lenktov turned to Fenella to see her reaction, but she was cold and expressionless. He pushed away the quilted jacket and felt the pulse on Zana's neck. Then he pulled up her eyelid.
- "No sign of life here", he said as he got up. - "Tonkin has ordered that we arrange it so that any traces of you go to Zana. In an investigation, hotel service and airline personnel may remember you. But it will never be possible to find your right identity, so we can count on the CIA swallowing the misleading information and accepting that you have ended your life here, even if it is actually Zana Jankaan. In a deserted place like this, it is unlikely that anyone will find the body until we are safe".

Lenktov picked up the cracked glasses and pressed the glass against Zana's fingers. He noticed that at the same time he put a print of his shoe in the dirt in front of Fenella's bonfire.
- "You can go down the path towards the road and wait for me there. But let me get your watch and your jewelry first". He put the jewels and leather hat together with the watch between the rocks behind her. At the same time he put the bag next to her together with the other rubber boot and an umbrella from Fenella. Then he emptied the rest of the contents of Fenella's gas bottle as well as the remains of a liqueur bottle over the clothes and the rubber boots. He took a few steps back and picked up the container with naphtha from under his armpit. The figure in front of him was still lifeless in a sitting position. He looked for Fenella, who had disappeared in the woods, and at the same

time noticed as the clouds drifted across the area. With a quick twist of his wrist, he let the fluid spread over the figure in front of him. He grabbed a matchbox, lit a match and let it light the others at the same moment as he threw the whole burning box into the fire. The flames struck like a little inferno and the heat pushed him back towards the forest. On his way between the trees, Lenktov did not notice the cramped figure move weakly and backwards with its head down between the stones.

Fenella waited by the road. They looked back, but could not distinguish smoke from fog. Fenella looked inquiringly at him and Lenktov nodded.

In the slightly downhill terrain, the hike back to the car was easier than it was going up. They met almost no people on the way up the valley.
- "We'll have to stop in the storage on the railroad before we leave", Lenktov breathed, while they were standing next to each other. - "The impression of the sunglasses is the only link we have between the suitcases and Zana if you have done a proper job".

They spent no more than 20 minutes getting back to the car and Fenella quickly put the sunglasses in one of the bags in the storage. She wondered whether she should remove the newspaper with the message from Rome, but then thought it could take care of the impression of herself or Zana as southern, perhaps Italian, and thus proved to be dissuasive.

Less than an hour after they had left the scene in Isdalen valley, Fenella and Lenktov were in the car on the way east to the border with Sweden. At eight o'clock that evening they arrived at Kikut Fjellstove at Geilo, after driving along the Hardangerfjord and on the snow over Hardangervidda. Tromboli had found a place to stay the night that he thought suitable for Lenktov and his identity, as he himself was well known in several of the larger hotels.

Early the next morning they continued the long trip north of Oslo, via Kongsvinger and Karlstad in Sweden and to Stockholm via Ørebro. They passed the border without controls. That evening, the car drove south from Værmdø towards Hårsfjærden in Stockholm's archipelago. They continued for a about 10 kilometers further to Nyneshavn and rolled onto the narrow gravel road that Lenktov knew from previous visits to the country, the home to a Swedish-American couple. Exhausted by the long trip, Lenktov stopped the engine and turned off the lights. They were well taken care of, the car was driven into a garage and both slept through the next day.

Just past midnight, the night before Thursday, they were taken by a small boat to one of the outermost of the hundreds of islets in the area. Voltov's people were ready with a rubber boat and both of them got on board in the USSR's Vostok that dove right away to its ultimate depth and speed.

Captain Voltov greeted the two agents upon arrival, with hot tea and vodka. – "Perfect timing, perfect dining!" he said in non-perfected English while standing triumphantly in front of a table laden with food.

Soon the Vostok was within the seabed limit beyond Tallinn in Estonia, and Fenella and Lenktov were transferred to a waiting cruiser and then on by helicopter and a small aircraft from Tallinn to Leningrad. Voltov set the course south to a waiting position north of the Baltic Sea.

After spending a few hours in a military transport plane, Fenella and Lenktov were, late in the evening, received by smiling Tonkin at the Moscow airport. At 8:00 AM Friday, November 27, the Defense Command and the Navy Over Commando were busy copying and distributing the material from Fenella. Bahria and Karlovich had duly congratulated Tonkin on the operation and informed the party secretary about the development so far.

Time ran out for Conahan who did not find any trace of Zana and by Wednesday had already received two phone calls from by an impatient Secretary-General. Since Monday, NATO had prepared itself for the worst, and on Thursday morning their biggest operation ever was taken down. All physical and operational positions throughout the fleet were abandoned and deleted and new strategic and tactical operations plans were issued. On Friday, November 27. all previous data was worthless.

Conahan was not completely dissatisfied with the result. Thanks to the investigation, the crisis was averted. Late Thursday afternoon just before he decided to leave Bergen, a message from a contact in Tallinn said that a man and a woman, similar to the description of Zana and Watson, had arrived by plane in a helicopter and flown on to Leningrad.

He shrugged his shoulders saying, - "It does not matter where they are now". Four days later he shook his head confusedly and looked again at the message about the discovery and the description of an unknown dead woman in the Isdalen valley in Bergen. He did not doubt that this was Zana and quickly asked the leadership in the CIA to ensure that NATO and Interpol prevented the police in Norway from unnecessarily revealing her identity and relationship with the CIA and KGB.

Tonkin, who was still happy, and unaware of NATO's recent disposals, received the same information that the woman was not identified on the telex from the embassy in Oslo on Tuesday morning and was gladly on his way to inform the party secretary that the operation Isotopsy had not yet been revealed.

The joy was short-lived. Late Friday afternoon, NATO's listening stations in northern Norway confirmed that they had decoded the Russian message that the order for going on full alert to Soviet forces for an attack was withdrawn.

Back in Rome at the beginning of December, following the activities in Flensburg and Bergen, Watson had previously received coverage after hearing about the questioning of the Swedish couple in Værmdø in connection with Tromboli's visit in October. Watson had introduced him to the Swedes and his American friends, as Watson knew them from his time of study at the Massachusetts Institute of Technology. Tonkin told him about the search of his house in Milan and asked him to "keep it down and low" and not maintain any contact through the Montessori school. The article about the school in Dagbladet found in the dead woman's suitcase could also help the Americans "smell" a connection between the three episodes. None of the three, Zana, Fenella, or Tromboli, had heard of Rome, and he felt a certain discomfort at the thought that something could have gone wrong.

A phone call to the Warnemann yard in Flensburg had disturbed him even more. The account name indicated that Gerber probably had an accident while driving from Flensburg to Hamburg and had driven off the road. His condition was unstable and he ad been given sickleave for an indefinite period. There appeared to have been burglaries in the car and he had reported the accident to the insurance company. He also said that two police officers had been in the office and asked for both Gerber and Watson. Watson shivered and his upper body shook. He quickly decided to get lost in Sicily.

Romboli was already in Finland after leaving Hurtigruten in Tromsø. From there, further assistance was provided via Skibotn and Zana's route of Tonkin's people in Finland and Norway had brought new orders at the arrival in Trondheim.

On a mild spring day in early February 1971, Lippke's photograph fell from a letter and down on a table in front of Fenella and Kelly where they sat overlooking Odessa's most beautiful setting. In the church book as pictured, one could easily see that it was written: at 11:45. Unknown woman. GL. 00, number 00, grave 01. Møhlendal".

Bergen, February 1971

On the way out of the funeral at Møhlendal Cemetery, Berger and Seland joined Thurmann, the head of Kripos (Specialist Crime Directorate). Both were clearly exhausted by the end of the two-month exploration in vain. The criminal boss was better off.
"Yes, yes, guys, that's it! All this work and then we just end up with a confused woman who was tired of life. But nevertheless, there is no doubt that we have gained considerable experience and that you all have done a fantastic job. The matter is now out of our hands." The two officers exchanged a look but said nothing for a while.
"This is not the end, if you ask me", Berger told Seland on his way to the car.
"That guy did not make it any easier for us. Why in the hell did he really stop us in Trondheim? And what about the Germans who were interrogated at Hotel Neptun"?
"Forget it! It is over now". Seland pulled up his collar and lit a cigarette.
"If something comes up, we will not be able to follow the tracks. It's been a long time since we should have realized that intelligence is not police work"!
"Ha! No, let's come back to everyday murder, robbery and morality before anyone suspects us of thinking for ourselves."
Seland sat in the Ford Consul and waved at Berger before he drove away. On his way past the train station, his thoughts reluctantly returned to the case. The fact that they could not find a single trace after sending inquiries and pathology reports over almost the whole world was a mystery. The attitude of the Kripos people also felt strange and uncomfortable.
The hundreds of inquiries from people who in retrospect remembered a situation they believed was related to the death was a little blurred, almost as if the case fit too well. Kripos perhaps knew more than they gave an impression of, but Seland believed that only POT could rely on information he or Kripos did not know. It was not a good feeling to give up the matter as unresolved regarding the identity of the woman, without

any answer to almost anything. Not least after hundreds, not to say thousands of interrogations and interviews!

- "Bahh" he murmured and threw the cigarette stump out of the window just as the car passed the taxi station and as he frowned as he got a slight glimpse of taxi 5129, which was empty.

Back home he brought in the newest edition of the Dagbladet newspaper. He didn't pay attention to a story on the front page about a German spy beeing shot by Russian intelligence people on the Norwegian side of the border, after having tried to enter Russia illegally.

Ten years later, at the police department in Bergen, Seland suddenly turned around in the office chair and thoughtfully said to Berger, - "There was damned little point in making a zinc coffin. Nobody ever missed her!"

Printed in Great Britain
by Amazon

21806857R00057